WHEN BOTH WORLDS MEET

By

Mungoni Manoge

PJ NTSOANE
P.O. Box 941, Lebowakgomo 0737
+2771 505 2333
POLOKWANE, LIMPOPO PROVINCE, RSA

Published in 2015

ISBN: 978-0-9922330-2-0

This is dedicated to those who love peace and justice.

Foreword

Mungoni Manoge's real name is Photoane Jeffrey Ntsoane. Mungoni Manoge is a pen-name that echoes his clan name Bakone ba Manoge, part of the baKoni tribes found in the northern parts of South Africa. They are the same family known as Angoni in Central Africa and amaNguni in Southern Africa.
(Oral history)

NB: Mungoni Manoge is totally opposed to discrimination on any basis including tribe, race, religion or gender
Names used in this novel are fictitious and in no way refer to any personality in the real world whatsoever.

1

When both worlds meet, sparks are bound to fly. These sparks could either be constructive or destructive. In science opposites attract and thus the resultant chemical reaction emits a by-product. This could be something that ushers in progress to the human race. In certain instances the sparks set off an explosion that makes the human race revert to atavism. This often occurs when racial bigots are forced by circumstances beyond or within their control to vie for scarce resources or power.

Sometimes the consequence of a bitter situation becomes a blessing in disguise. It is very rare for positive results to be reaped without a major compromise by either side of the parties involved. Racial prejudice is a major nagging problem that the world is grappling with. Some people are trying their best to mitigate its brute facts while others perpetuate it by becoming the proverbial ostriches.

Rampho is one of the many men who find themselves in the eye of the storm of an untenable situation where both worlds meet. This frail old man is sitting under a huge mango tree that barely bears fruits anymore. He remembers when he reaped the first fruits in the olden days. The tree was still the appropriate size. He recalls how the apple of his eye, his little beautiful daughter, Mpho could pick the fleshy and juicy fruits with ease. She used to love the mangoes so much that she would always tenaciously monitor the progress of their ripeness. She would even designate some for her own consumption. She made sure that the tree was well watered because she didn't want the growth of her succulent juicy darlings disturbed.

The mango tree has now grown too big and out of control. The old man, Rampho feels that besides the patchy shade, the tree offers no other tangible delicacy. Mampho, who is showing signs of ageing, complains incessantly about trash she has to sweep every morning as a result of the leaves that it sheds so generously. Mampho wants nothing more than to see the tree cut.

"Papa, please find someone to cut this tree or I will cut it myself. All it does is litter my yard. I do not have strength to deal with its projectile missiles. These weak bones of mine!" exclaims Mampho. Rampho feels that his manhood is being challenged by his woman of ages. No man who is worth his salt wants his personal territory invaded. That always precipitates a retreat to the manly fortress. He shakes his mountain of a head, waggles a finger at his wife who is standing with hands akimbo, looking at him.

"Watch your tongue, woman! That is my department," he says threateningly, "I have also realised that this tree has outgrown its usefulness. It has to be pruned to the right size, but not destroyed. It is like these children of nowadays who have grown too big for their parents and have lost touch with reality. One also thinks of politicians who think that they are untouchable once they are given a sit in the upper echelons. They become big headed and succumb to the temptation of recalcitrance. They tend to delude themselves that they are God sent," he retorts with a sneer.

"*Yebo* Papa, you can say that again. This world has changed for the worse. If it is not the wayward, it is the salient industrialised nations with their manipulative tactics which cause unbearable heat and diseases," replies Mampho.

"The world is overloaded and confused," says Rampho, taking a deep sigh.

Rampho sits and gazes into the distant horizon, he seems swamped in thoughts. He occasionally shakes his snow-white head. He appears to be absorbed in something too bitter for his mind's consumption. It is about the cell phone call he received recently. It was from his only child and daughter, Mpho. He had not had a special call from her in the past six months. She is married to a man of a different race and culture. She met him while at university. She is a qualified advocate since she obtained her master's degree in law abbreviated (LLM). She is a career woman. To him she will always be his little daughter, the dawn of his dreams and the apple of his eye.

He reminisces about the day his lovely wife gave birth to her:

She went to this dilapidated blacks-only hospital in the rural homeland where he grew up and was employed as a teacher. When he met his wife at the maternity ward where the new mothers resided, she was all smiles.

She said, "My love, we have a lovely daughter. She has taken your eyes and lips." Rampho's heart was jumping with joy in his chest. He was stricken dumb for a while. He was suddenly a parent, a father. He named her Mpho, which means a gift from God.

"I thank God and the ancestors for this precious gift. Thank you my lovely wife for this gift. You have done well Mahlako," he said with tears welling in his eyes. He was ecstatic. It was like the first rays of a new day and age. He gave his wife a hug and a kiss. She looked frail despite her radiant face. She was over the moon.

Since this was her first child, she was strong for a young mother who had given birth a few hours ago. He wished he could have been there when all that happened, but for his traditional beliefs. He would not dare venture anywhere near that deep secret. That is how he grew up. His father and elders always said that child birth was women's dark secret. He always wondered why that was the case because he was taught about reproduction in his secondary school lessons and besides, he was a Biology teacher himself. He had seen a number of young male maternity nurses. He always wondered why a male nurse should be called a sister. "Is a sister not supposed to be a female sibling? So much for equality," he mused. He even toyed with the idea of taking the department to court. "Is this not another form of discrimination? Why are male nurses not called brothers instead?" he ruminated. He tried to enquire of some nurses and doctors but none could provide a credible answer. "Why am I concerned about other people's business? If the people concerned do not seem to have a problem with it and enjoy attainment of the status or being called by that incongruous title, man, let the sleeping dogs lie," he said to himself. He wondered what his father and grandfather would say if they saw a maternity ward being overseen by male staff. They would regard that as taboo and would judge those young men as womanish.

Unfortunately Rampho was not allowed to see his daughter on that first day. He was eager to see and hold his blessing in his own hands. That would make him fulfilled. The staff there said that only the mothers and the staff were allowed into the room where the new-born babies were kept. He reluctantly obliged as that was the hospital policy. They also had policy at his place of work that visitors observed. He would also feel undermined if visitors did as they wished at his school. Rampho could only conjure up a picture of his beloved little girl based on the mother's description. They did not have cell phones at the time. Life was not as fast-paced as in the modern times. The waiting for the mother to be discharged and bring the precious blessing to the glare of the outside world seemed eternal. He went to the nearby town of Heitersburg to buy baby clothes and other presents.

The day he had been waiting for dawned. The baby was finally coming home. He hurried to the mother's room but a rude awakening was waiting for him. He could not go anywhere near the mother and the baby. It is tradition. He would only have access to the baby after a week long wait. "Terrible! Is this not one other form of discrimination?" he mumbled. He felt he was entitled to see and hold his own baby. Not when there was a conservative guard, Grandmother Mahlako sitting with the young mother. They even put a stick across the doorstep as a sign of no entry. Rampho pleaded with the old woman for laxity of the traditional rule but to no avail. They accepted his presents and bellowed his praise poem. He felt a tickling sensation down his spine as the old woman related the heroic deeds of his ancestors. He felt he could pick up a spear and face the fiercest of enemies on the battlefield. He came from a lineage of great warriors. He could only catch a glimpse of his precious daughter through a window. Perhaps the mother was empathetic. She knew how her man was dying to see his daughter and staged a subtle tantalising gimmick.

"It is the time for women to flex their muscles. At a time like this they enjoy seeing men on their knees pleading for mercy to have a taste or glimpse of what they desire," said Nkwe, Rampho's father.

"You have hit the mark, son! At a crucial moment of desire, one who holds the key to satiation gets personal satisfaction from acknowledgement by those who want. Sometimes a person in an advantageous position would play a little god. The disadvantaged are made to feel the pinch, that way they learn to be thankful and the giver's ego is elevated," said Rampho's grandfather, Ntona.

"It is unfair. Is it not true that blessed is the hand that gives and the humble are elevated by God?" asked Rampho.

"It is a saying. It depends on to whom it will be referring at any given time," said Ntona.

2

Mpho's marriage to Funkel, a sturdy handsome young man from an affluent suburb near the coastal city of Cape Town, was not a bed of roses anymore. It had become so rocky that many close friends wondered why they were still together anyway. The strained relationship had permeated their families who resorted to hurling derogatory labels at one another.

People had initially always thought that theirs was a marriage designed in heaven. They were regarded as an ideal couple envied by all and sundry. Some people thought their marriage epitomised nation building in a country that was grappling with a galling after-taste of institutionalised racism. There were spurious racial spats from both sides of the families. What went wrong? None was prepared to take the blame lest they ended with an egg on the face.

It had not always been like that in paradise. Theirs was what one could describe as love at first sight. The two lovebirds met on campus while they were both students at Laager University. Mpho was this innocent rural girl who knew nothing about dating. Funkel, a typical city sly, was smitten head over heels when he first laid his blue eyes on the brownie. She was wearing her tight denims with a blouse that exposed her navel. What she was wearing exposed her voluptuous essentials that left the poor dude agape. His heart was pounding against his chest so hard that he thought everyone on campus could hear or notice its cage popping up and down. He ran out of the library in case all that was only a passing whim. He ran straight to the cafeteria and ordered a strong black coffee to calm his sorry nerves. The image of the black beauty stuck in his mind like a super glue. He thought he saw her mouth-watering face in the cup. He was unconsciously salivating. He only came to his senses when a trickle of saliva ran down his chin. After taking a few gulps he ran straight to his room, flung himself onto the bed and sprawled there to ponder.

That night sleep eluded him. All he could attain was staring at the ceiling and incessant tossing. It seemed he was the prisoner of that African charm. He never thought he would look at a black girl that way. Not if he was from a white conservative family and neighbourhood. When he grew up he was taught that blacks were sub-human and their association with whites had to be as the master and servant or subordinate. He had never had a black person for a friend. The only blacks that he had known were Sara, the maid, and Jan, the gardener. The two seemed ignorant and were patronised by his folks. They were always apologetic and thankful for a mere friendly gesture or a little hand-out. That corroborated his father's claim.

He then became a fellow student with blacks and sat with them in classes. He was astounded by the intelligence and command of European languages displayed by some of the black students.

The next morning Funkel woke up tired and a little perplexed. He quickly took a shower and sped to the dining hall where he had his breakfast. He was acting strangely for a guy known to be a chatterbox. He seemed taciturn and withdrawn. His friend, Jaas noticed that there was something wrong with his friend. He knew him very well. The two were from the same neighbourhood. They attended the same church, played for the same rugby club and went to the same schools.

"Hey, dude, are you alright?" enquired Jaas.

"Yeah, everything is fine dude, I am only worried about the Physics assignment that is due next week," retorted Funkel dismissively.

"Since when do you have a problem with a Physics task?" asked Jaas.

"You have always been the brainiest and the whole neighbourhood knew that you were good at almost all the subjects," added Jerome, one of his friends sitting next to him.

"No, it is only in your twisted imagination. This guy cheated in most of the tests that we wrote. Didn't you know that he is an astute copycat?" said Louis teasingly.

"You guys don't know what you are talking about," replied Funkel, "at this institution we have this Professor Mazwane. He is also Dean of the Faculty. He regards the faculty as his fiefdom. What makes me boil with anger is that he thrives in frustrating students. He makes sure that he plucks the fruits before they become ripe if you know what I mean. He is on the devilish mission of destroying students' future. He subscribes to the sick self-fulfilling prophecy that Physics is difficult and meant only for the highly intelligent. He relishes seeing disappointment and despair in the faces of those who rely on him," said Funkel giving out a contemptuous sigh of desperation.

"This sounds like he is a sadist black racist," commented Jaas, "their ilk become power-drunk once they assume a higher position. Obviously he is pampering children of his side-kicks or sells courses for you know what. These people make me sick to say the least," said Jaas.

"No, he is a sadist that knows no colour. He once astounded a group of students who had been waiting for him at his office to enquire about their applications for a retest when he blatantly told them that he was not there to save anyone's future. The students looked astounded. They were so shocked when he disdainfully hollered at them to stop wasting his time. He felt like a god at that moment. It is paradoxical because he is one of whom blacks look up to as role models. Tell me if that is racism if he has to flex his languid muscles at his own people like that," said Funkel.

"Maybe that is tribalism," joked Jerome and everybody chuckled.

"Anyway, it is fine if we have powerful blacks who deal with the spoilt 'so-called' formerly disadvantaged," said Jaas.

Funkel suddenly kept quiet. He seemed enmeshed in daydreaming. He silently prayed not to meet that girl he saw the previous day. He didn't trust his own feelings and how he would react if he ever saw her again. He was busy brooding, oblivious to the fact that his friends had already left. He quickly stood up and went up to his room which was on the fifth floor of the hostel.

©PJ Ntsoane

He later joined the hustle and bustle of students rushing to their various destinations. He went to the administration block to fix his meals card. There were several students standing in the queue to the administrative clerk. He sauntered to join them. He was allergic to standing in long queues. His eyes were scanning those in the queue searching for someone he could manipulate into allowing him to squeeze in under the pretext that he had been there before. While doing his cunning scanning, he bumped against the last person standing in the queue. Funkel nearly fainted when he realised that the person he collided with was the girl he had seen the day before.

"Sorry, that was clumsy of me! I didn't mean to... to be rude nor cause any harm. It was an accident. I am terribly sorry. Please accept my apology," stuttered Funkel.

"Okay, apology accepted. You need to look where you are going, though," replied the brown angel with a smile. Her teeth were so white and perfect that Funkel's heart nearly melted with desire.

"My name is Funkel," he said, stretching his trembling hand out for a handshake.

"I am Mpho," she retorted, turning away. She wouldn't dare shake his hand. She felt a chill down her spine. Her heart was racing. Her forehead and palms were sweaty.

"Can I buy you a cup of coffee sometime?" asked Funkel sheepishly.

"I don't drink coffee," Mpho replied curtly.

"I could buy you anything, ice-cream or cocktail. Please!" said Funkel, not taking no for an answer.

"Since you insist, ice cream will be fine," said the young woman shyly. They exchanged cell phone numbers. The intercom called: 'Next please!' It was time for Mpho to be attended to. Funkel stood there like a statue marvelling at nature's perfection as she walked swinging her hip from side to side.

Funkel suddenly became vivacious and was all smiles. He looked like a young boy who had just scored his first 'tri' in a big rugby competition. His face lit up. He was wearing a silly smile on his face all day. His friends noticed the sudden positive change in him.

"Whoever is responsible for that metamorphosis deserves a round of applause. Welcome back, dude," said Jaas patting him on the back.

"You will never know," replied Funkel, with a smile.

While in his room Funkel fiddled with his cell phone, anxious to call the girl he so madly had fallen in love with. He ultimately gathered courage and dialled.

When it was ringing he nearly dropped it because he was so frightened.

"Hello, this is Mpho. Who am I speaking to?" there was silence. Funkel was chickening out. "Funkel, is that you?" asked Mpho, who was astounded. She had not saved his cell phone number.

"Ye... yes Mpho, Hi," he said timidly, "shall we get together this Saturday afternoon for a drink at the cafeteria?" asked Funkel, trembling with fear. He was glad he was alone in the room.

"Fine, what time?" asked Mpho.

"Well, will 15H00 be fine?" he suggested, now a little bit composed.

"Okay, see you then," she said.

The date went well. They chatted about almost everything: the courses they were studying, their chosen career path, sport, the hi-tech and the economy. They were both fascinated by each other's knowledge. Funkel took Mpho's hand and wrapped it in both his. Mpho withdrew her hand quickly and stood up. "Sorry, I have to go," she said, unable to look him in the eyes. "Alright, I have really enjoyed this. Can we do it again some other time?" he asked her with a smile.

"Yeah, thank you. I have to go. See you around," she said turning towards the door. Funkel stood up and left. When he was on the way he jumped and punched the air with excitement.

 Mpho had this strange feeling in her gut. She realised that it must be love. She had never fallen in love with anyone before. "This must be the one I have been waiting for. Destiny has worked its magic hand," she thought. Her mother had always told her to beware of smooth talkers. As a born again Christian herself she was not intending to fall in love with anyone unless she was sure he was the right man. Her father, as a traditionalist also believed in chastity until marriage was concluded. He was a very strict man. He sometimes threatened that he would disown a child who misbehaved. This princess would not dare invite the wrath of her doting father. She knew how protective and fussy he was when it came to her wellbeing. If he caught wind of her escapades on campus he would go ballistic. Her suitor's parents were both conservative. They would both have a seizure if they knew what their boy was up to. They had unshaken trust in their boy.

3

The two strange lovers' relationship became the talk of campus. Friends on both sides of the fence on campus scolded their respective friend for betrayal. They felt sold out to the enemy by their trusted one. They set up meetings to court martial the culprits.

The first meeting to materialise was that of Funkel's camp. Jaas gathered his friends at his own room. It was on the fifth floor of Block D of the male residences. Everybody was curious about this impromptu meeting. Jaas was not smiling and joking as always. "Hey Jaas, what's wrong? Has someone died? You look so gloomy," enquired Jerome, seriously concerned.

"Hold your horses, dude. I will tell you everything soon," said Jaas, with a frown on his face.

"Whatever it is that you called us here for must be the hell of tidings," added Funkel.

"Sure it is," retorted Jaas, "guys, my heart is bleeding with disappointment," he said curtly.

"Stop speaking in parables. You are not the second coming," teased Jerome.

"Let me stop dilly-dallying and go straight to the main point of our gathering here today," he said sipping a glass of water. He turned off the radio that was on his reading desk.

"This concerns rumours that I have heard about our dear friend here, Funkel," he continued pointing at him with an open hand.

"What?" Funkel asked, seemingly startled.

"Don't interrupt!" ordered Jerome, "I was approached by Lizzy, that lovely girl from Johannesburg. She told me that she saw Funkel in the company of a black girl several times here on campus. She even saw them drinking coffee together at the cafeteria yesterday. She said the two looked cosy. Now I would like to know from you Funkel, if you know anything about that," Jaas said fiercely looking Funkel in the eyes.

"Since when is it your concern whom I go out with?" enquired Funkel angrily.

"It became *our* concern since you were born a *Boer seun*. We have to guard our moral values with our lives," said Jaas angrily.

"Guys, you are my friends not my parents," replied Funkel.

"What do you think your parents would say if they caught wind of this?" asked Jerome, "they would definitely disown you," he added.

"Dudes, I don't care who says what. I didn't choose to fall in love with her. You can go to hell if you have a problem with that," Funkel said poking at his friends with his finger.

"Hey *boet*, we have many beautiful girls of our own on campus. Why do you decide to denigrate yourself and embarrass us like this?" asked Jaas, now on his feet.

"If you don't find any white girl on campus attractive, I can take you to town. You will meet many of your own there," suggested Jerome, also standing up.

"Look guys, I don't know if you have heard me very well. Read my lips, I don't care!" shouted Funkel.

Love is tastier than anything delicious. It strums the strings of the heart and titillates the feelings of passion. The world of the admired one turns into a sweet haven.

Mpho was hanging out with her friends at the park on campus. It was Sunday afternoon and the girls had just returned from church. They were relaxing since they didn't have pressure of work to do.

"Girls, I have a secret to share with you," said Mpho, smiling from ear to ear.

"That must be a honey comb of a secret, chomza," replied Dineo, returning a smile.

"If it is sweet, let it out chomza. Let us have a taste of the honey you have for us," said Koketso.

"Girls, I think I have been swept off my feet," Mpho continued. The girls responded with a well-choreographed hand touching and a silly laughter.

"Come on, I can't bear the suspense, girl! Who is the lucky guy?" asked Dineo.

"Is he a Born Again as well?" asked Koketso, teasingly.

"Well, he is fine by my terms," said Mpho stroking her extension mane.

"You know we have high standards," said Dineo.

"Yeah, he surpasses your standards by far," replied Mpho, giggling a bit, "he is white," she added.

It was like the two friends had been hit by a thunder bolt. They remained agape for a minute. They stared at one another lost for words.

"What?" they asked in unison.

"Stop joking, you will give us heart attacks," said Dineo.

"His name is Funkel. He is tall, dark and handsome," said Mpho, bragging to her friends.

"You have just said he is white. How can he become dark? I have never seen a dark white person," teased Koketso.

"Maybe he is trying to tan his skin to look like an African," said Dineo. They laughed.

"You are silly. Whatever you say will not make any difference. I am in too deep," retorted Mpho.

"To err is human. You can still remedy the wrongs you have done by cordially ending this stupid relationship. Just say, it was a mistake and he will understand. After all, this is bound to end any time soon. Stop it while there is still time and avoid a heart-break," remarked Koketso.

"Come on Mpho, this person is not one of your own. You come from two different worlds. Wake up girl! What attracted you to him anyway? Was it his complexion or the shape of his European nose? Come on girlfriend, we have many African brothers on campus who have better features," said Dineo, showing concern.

"I hear you girls. I will end things next time we meet and I promise you. Besides, my parents will not approve of this relationship," said Mpho, trying to appease her friends.

There was another girl who was sitting close enough to overhear their conversation. She looked modern and was seen in the company of campus party groupies several times. She was known to be leading a rough life and she had been on campus for five years already. Rumour had it that she had been to other universities before Laager.

She was from a wealthy new black elite family that had connections in the higher echelons of government. Her family was famous for lucrative government tenders that they acquired easily. Her family members drove around in flashy imported cars. She felt the urge to intervene. "Sorry girls, I couldn't help eavesdropping. If I may add my voice to what you have just said, I mean if it is okay with you. You are being unfair to this girl," interjected Nogana.

"Hey *wena,* mind your own business. You have no right sticking your nose in our affairs," warned Dineo, pointing a threatening finger at Nogana.

"Nobody speaks to me like that. Watch your mouth you spoilt...," interrupted Nogana, "you claim to be Christians and civilised but you still promote racial hatred. Shame on you!" she exclaimed.

"We are only stating the facts here. We know how these white boys regard us, blacks. They use our sisters to experiment their wild fantasies. They do not truly love us that much," said Koketso.

"Look who is talking. You are wearing fake White and Indian people's hair, nails and eye lashes. You even use skin lighteners so you can look like whites. Is it not a question of envy or jealousy? Haven't you heard that love knows no colour? Maybe you wish the white boy had fallen in love with you instead. Have you ever heard of sour grapes?" said Nogana.

"Girls please, stop fighting over this trifle. I am the one who has the final say here, aren't I?" interrupted Mpho, standing up showing that it was time to go back to their hostel. It was almost time for dinner.

Nogana lit up her cigarette. She looked so angry that she felt like wringing the necks of those archaic girls. She grew up in the family that was supposedly involved in the *struggle*. Her family believed in non-racialism and non-discrimination. She heard her father talk about nation building and unity in diversity. She was taught to be magnanimous since the party that she belonged to advocated national reconciliation. She was perturbed by university students who were still caught in the old mentality of racial segregation. She thought that since institutionalised racism had been defeated there was no need to light up the embers of racial hatred. Instead the youth should strive to extinguish those embers that were still hot and menacing.

She realised there was still a lot of work to be done in exorcising those brainwashed by architects of racism. As an executive member of the Student Representative Council and an active member of the youth wing of Revolutionary Democratic Movement she felt that she was duty bound to take up political education as a priority in leadership caucuses. She saw

Mpho as a vehicle for attitude changes in their formerly whites-only Laager University. The community of this institution was still in the grip of racial prejudice.

Mpho hardly slept a wink that night. She had conflicting ideas about what transpired at the park. She was beginning to realise that her involvement with Funkel could cost her a lot. She could lose her friends and evoke the wrath of her parents. She picked up her cell phone and buzzed Funkel. He responded quickly.

"Hello, beautiful girl. I was thinking about you. I considered calling you but I thought I would disturb your peaceful night," said Funkel.

"Never mind, it would not have made any difference. My night had already been disturbed anyway. I could hardly fall asleep as well," responded Mpho.

"What is the matter my love? Is there something that troubles you or are you thinking about me?" asked Funkel.

"Yeah, it is complicated. Maybe we should meet and talk about it soon," said Mpho, sobbing and trying hard not to let Funkel become suspicious.

"Okay, see you tomorrow at our usual spot then. Have sweet dreams and they better be about me," said Funkel ending the call.

___4___

Jaas was being mischievous. He got hold of Funkel's father's mobile phone number and sent him an MMS showing Funkel in a cosy posture with Mpho. Funkel's father nearly had a heart attack when he saw the message. He thought maybe his son's friend was playing tricks on him. He hastily called his son on his mobile phone. Funkel had put his phone on voice mail because he was busy with a practical in the science laboratory. He was doing a Bachelor of Science Chemical Engineering. His father had high hopes for him and was always boasting to his friends about this well behaved and intelligent *Boer seun*. He was convinced that he had inculcated in him the values of his culture.

Funkel found his father's voice message and suddenly had a premonition that he was bubbling with anger. He was hesitant to give him a call. He reckoned he would call again if what he wanted to say was urgent. He carried on with his daily business as if nothing had happened. Late in the afternoon his cell phone rang. It was his father.

"Hey *mannetjie*, you have some serious explanation to do," said his father in an unusually slow voice.

"What have I done now?" asked Funkel, sounding a little perplexed.

"I sent you to Laager University to study not to frolic with savage girls," said Piet, reverting to his conservative self.

"Dad who told you such lies? You know I love education. I won't sacrifice it for anything," said Funkel, now sounding more concerned.

"I have reason to believe that you are dating an African girl. I have received an MMS from someone. It proves that beyond any reasonable doubt. Denying that will not help," said Piet, now furious.

"Who sent you that?" asked Funkel.

"I will not betray my reliable source. I want you to come home this weekend. Your mother and I would like to talk sense into your crazy head," concluded Piet and he abruptly ended the call.

Funkel was left agape. His heart was palpitating. He was wondering who could have sent an MMS to his father. He suspected one of his friends since they did not approve of his relationship with Mpho. They were the ones who had his parents' cell phone numbers. He thought that was only a storm in a tea cup that would soon fade out but he was mistaken. It was escalating into something serious. He was convinced that those opposed to their relationship were only making a mountain out of a mole hill. Why should a precious thing as love be unreasonably made to seem so traumatic? Everybody in the country was talking about reconciliation yet their actions depicted the contrary.

He found it hard to comprehend these people's reaction because it contradicted their religious beliefs. The whole world was hyped up about national reconciliation and peace that was achieved amicably in his country. He felt anger overpowering him. He clenched his fists, tightened his teeth and took a deep breath.

He opened the door to his room and slumped on his bed. He closed his eyes and said a short prayer: "Lord, didn't you create man in your own image. All men irrespective of the colour of their skin are in your own image. Why can't these people stop persecuting us? We never meant for all these to happen when we fell in love. Please guide us," said Funkel, opening his eyes. He felt as if a large boulder had been lifted off his shoulders.

That weekend Mpho decided to go home as well. She had not seen her family in six weeks. She was longing to sit and chat with her mother and catch up. The two were inseparable. They seemed like the closest of friends. Mpho did not keep any secrets from her mother. Her mother knew her like the back of her own hand. She could immediately tell when she was not feeling well. She quickly detected that she was not her true self.

"Mpho, what is wrong girl?" she asked.

"Why do you ask Mama?" replied Mpho, showing surprise.

"I know you. You are my baby. I raised you, remember?" she said emphatically.

Mpho cast her eyes on the floor. She didn't know how to tell her mother what was gnawing her conscience. She wished she could evaporate or disappear beneath the tiles on the floor and let someone do the talking for her. She had spoken to her mother about anything and it was easy all the time. She wondered why it was a steep hill for her to lay bare what was happening in her life.

"You know you can trust me. You can talk to me about anything," Mampho continued.

"I know Mom. It is just that this one is unusual. It has never happened to me before. I know you are going to be angry with me," said Mpho, with a sombre look on her face.

"You know I cannot be angry with my sweet baby. What is it girl?" said Mampho reassuring her daughter.

"Mom, I have met this boy on campus and we... we are dating," said Mpho hesitantly. She stole the look on her mother's face. She thought she would see her darkening with anger. Mampho remained silent, looked in the far distance for a while and took a deep breath. Mpho felt like she had waited for eternity.

"Please, say something Mom. I will not be surprised if you disown me. I am terribly sorry. Please forgive me, Mom," pleaded Mpho.

"What is his name?" asked Mampho, inaudibly. Mpho didn't hear her mother clearly.

"Mom?" called out Mpho, a little jumpy. Mampho raised her hand to scratch her itchy scalp. Mpho ducked. Her mother fixed her eyes on her. She was breathing heavily. Mpho was trembling and her hands were on her cheeks.

"I say, what is his name?" repeated Mampho, now a smile appearing on her beautiful face.

"His name is Funkel, he..." said Mpho.

"Funkel, what kind of a name is that?" interrupted Mampho, looking at Mpho with a frown.

"He is white," said Mpho.

"He is what?" asked Mampho, seemingly shocked.

"He is a real nice guy, Mom. He is a true gentleman," said Mpho, now showing signs of being less tense.

"What do you know about being a gentleman?" asked Mampho. Mpho could only giggle. She read fiction books and watched movies about love stories. She wondered what her mother took her for.

"It is fine, darling. As long as you are sure about what you are doing and happy, I will not stand in your way," said Mampho.

As they were busy laughing Rampho entered the room. They kept quiet. He sensed there was something mischievous about their conversation. He looked at them, shook his head and smiled.

"You two, I hope you are not plotting my downfall. I feel outnumbered in this house. I have to employ a secret intelligence agent to monitor your clandestine activities," he said jokingly.

"Women have the power to disarm the fiercest of enemies. It is a gift from God. We will infiltrate and disintegrate your intelligence agents," said Mampho with laughter.

"I know. Great men fell as a result of irresistible charm of beauty," he said, "by the way, how is my little angel?" he continued.

"I am fine Dad. How are you my hero?" Mpho asked.

"I am doing well for an old man like myself," said Rampho.

©PJ Ntsoane

Rampho was glad to see his darling daughter. He looked at his daughter and felt pride rising in his chest. She has grown into such an intelligent young woman of good morals and values. He was thinking that whoever was going to win her hand in marriage would have to be compatible pound for pound. He didn't wish for her daughter, who was properly raised, to be married to an abusive man who regarded women as his personal property. Those are the ones who would be as sweet as lambs during their courting days and once they consummated their marriage, they churn out their devilish self. Rampho reckoned that was the reason for a large number of divorce cases wasting the state money.

It really boggles one's mind why people who seemed so much in love would suddenly become sworn enemies who are at daggers drawn. They would be wishing upon each other worst calamity or malady. What happened to their famous swearing: 'for better or worse'? He wondered. Rampho dreaded such tragedy befalling his beloved daughter. He even toyed with the thought of having to obtain a profile of whoever would come to his house to seek his daughter's hand in marriage. The prospective son-in-law would be subjected to stringent scrutiny. He would strangle the man who would ill-treat the apple of his eye. He had seen men and women who treated their partners like trash. They first cheated on their partners, abused and then dumped them like rotten apples. He was wondering why people get married to ultimately hurt each other. He considered that to be pure sadism. He had witnessed tragic separations which ended in cold blooded murder. Some of the murderers were the main reason for the collapse of their own marriages. He wondered why would a person cheat on his or her partner and still refuse to set them free. Is it not logical that if a person has grown tired of someone else's company they should part ways amicably?

He thought of sharing this life lesson with his daughter to prepare her for adulthood but balked in compliance with his inviolable traditional values. A man would not discuss sex or love relationship issues with a girl. It was out of question. If Mpho was a boy he would be bound to share manhood issues with him after his return from initiation school. In his tradition a boy earns the right to share ideas with grown men only when he returned from the mountain school. It is paradoxical because in his capacity as learners' counsellor he was wont to say children could discuss whatever pertains to sex and adolescence issues with both their parents if they were available. He couldn't walk the talk in this case. Rampho couldn't suspect any mishap in his daughter at that instant. It remained the mother-daughter's little secret.

5

Funkel boarded the evening flight to his coastal city home. It is a one hour flight. When on board the first-class plane he inserted his iPod headphones into his ears and listened to his favourite rock music. The music soothed his tortured mind. The shrilling voice of the singer, the squeaking guitars and thumbing kick drum hypnotised him into a world of fantasy. He imagined how peaceful the world would be if everybody listened to rock music.

He found his father's driver waiting for him at the airport. He quickly carried the small suitcase that contained his valuables including a few books and an expensive laptop computer. He was whisked off in his father's luxury German made car. He fell asleep on the road since his companion was almost taciturn.

When he arrived at home he found his father waiting for him in the lounge. His mother had already gone to bed.

"Hello, young man. You have arrived," said Piet turning the TV volume low to enable conversation to flow.

"Good evening Papa. I couldn't wait another second. What you said disturbed me," replied Funkel, not as radiant as usual.

"Let us leave that for tomorrow. I am exhausted. I need to retire. I was only waiting for you to arrive home," said Piet standing up and walking up the stairs.

"Okay, Dad, I am also tired. I need a warm bath before I go to bed," said Funkel stretching and yawning. They bade each other goodnight and parted.

Funkel took a soothing bath, grabbed a sandwich and went upstairs to his bedroom. He lay on his bed for a while and decided to call his girlfriend before he slept. His father happened to be passing in the passage when he heard that his son was on the phone. He went to his son's door and pressed his ear against it. He could only hear Funkel say, "Sweet heart, I love only you. Take care. I will see you on campus." He concluded that he was talking to his black girl friend. He hardly slept a wink that night thinking about how he was going to convert his son's obsession. He realised that it was going to be a mammoth task to achieve his objective. He needed to think hard and act swiftly if he was to achieve positive results.

The next morning Funkel didn't wake up early. His father was anxious to talk to him. He sent the house maid Annah to wake him up. When Funkel came downstairs his father had already had his breakfast.

"Good morning, Dad," said Funkel as he opened a refrigerator to take out a pint of milk for breakfast. Piet looked at his son and greeted him accordingly.

"You overslept. If this is how you sleep at Laager I am afraid you will not bring back the degree," said Piet teasingly.

"Don't worry Dad, I am the best," said Funkel reassuring his father.

"I hope the best you are talking about is not concerning charming of girls," quipped Piet.

"No, Paps. How could you think that?" asked Funkel.

"I don't know what to think anymore after what transpired. I am still in shock," said Piet with a serious countenance.

"About that, I don't know who that sick person is who sent you such nonsense," said Funkel looking a little uncomfortable.

"I don't know but pictures down lie. I have no doubt that it is true. Thanks to the creative genes of white people. Where would these beautiful things have come from? This is a fast paced world and we made it that way. We civilised the continents of the savages, the Americas, Asia and Africa," said Piet with a sneer on his face.

"Dad, you know what you are saying is not true. People in those continents had their own civilisations.

White people destroyed them during colonisation,"
replied Funkel, taking a spoonful of corn flakes and
munching away at his favourite breakfast cereal. He
always enjoyed waking up to a bowl of crispy cereal.

"Do you call those civilisations? They were drab
institutions waiting for the white man's genius and
technological might. That is why they fell to us so
easily," said Piet with a foolish smug grin.

"What you are saying is dangerous, Dad. You must not
forget that we are currently living in a democratic
dispensation. All people are equal in the eyes of the
law," said Funkel.

"Equal my foot. The white man will never be equal to
a black person. God didn't create us that way!"
exclaimed Piet showing signs of irritation.

"Do you remember the 'Winds of Change' speech?
You have become an old ostrich. It is futile denying
reality," said Funkel wittingly.

"The only changes that will happen are those that the
white man approves of. We only want changes that
will not disturb the status quo. We have created
lieutenants who will look out for our interests in the
top hierarchy of ruling parties in the whole world.
They have to toe the line while we are in the
background to reap the benefits. You know we are
geniuses. We strategically create a small affluent class

that will have so much to lose if they deviate from our agenda. They are forced to depend on and work with us," said Piet, taking out his favourite cigarette.

"You are playing into the hands of political demagogues. We don't want to experience genocide. Those in power have the capacity to resort to inhuman retaliatory acts of violence if provoked," said Funkel.

"We have international institutions that act as watchdogs. Besides we created guns, bombs, tanks, war planes and other sophisticated weaponry. We even train their intelligence service personnel. If they attempt any nonsense we will bomb them to extinction. We make sure that we sustain military prowess as a deterrent. Our brothers in Europe are very innovative when it comes to warfare. We are always a thousand steps ahead. We only let these people know and access so much. We are very cautious and will not totally trust them. I am only glad that they are so naïve to celebrate these weapons that helped us conquer them. I cannot help it but chuckle whenever I see them using these guns for gun salute during national ceremonies like the opening of parliament. I can only say, 'good boys' to them," replied Piet.

"Dad, we need one another. Europeans would not have been able to develop their countries without ample resources and markets from these continents that you are now denigrating. Remember that colonial settlers were landless peasants in their home countries before they came to these places and usurped natives' ancestral heritage. European protectionism was not helping those brothers of yours until they decided to colonise. Indigenous people in these continents have been magnanimous and you must meet them half way," Funkel quipped. His father kept quiet for a while, he seemed to be thinking about something serious.

"Whites provided education to those people. We have created for them a vantage-point of viewing the world. That is the white-man's world. Therefore their angle of reasoning should be favourable to us. We call the shots here. Whoever thinks otherwise or conjures up equality between blacks and whites must be dealt with abruptly. We cannot afford those who intend to muddy the waters and pollute the minds of our servants. You have to come with me to a meeting this afternoon," said Piet.

"What is the meeting about?" asked Funkel.

"It is a Folks Party meeting. The president is speaking today. It is going to be a huge gathering," said Piet, his face lighting up.

"I am not a member of that party. How am I supposed to heed the call? Besides, political gatherings bore me to the bone. Politicians are so pretentious. They tell you one thing today and say that you misunderstood them the following day. It is an insult to our intelligence," said Funkel shaking his head.

"Do not compare him with these corrupt African leaders who have no one iota of honesty in their genes. Our leader is a truthful one. What he says is inspired by God. He says nothing but the truth. You must come and hear him speak. You will feel the spirit of Heavens descend upon you," said Piet with confidence.

Funkel reluctantly accompanied his father to the Folks Party meeting. When he arrived at the stadium it was a hype of activities. People were clad in their party colours and the stadium was reverberating with song. The young and old seemed in the grip of riveting excitement. When the leader's arrival was announced the stadium rose in deafening rupture.

"Long Live! The Lion of the South, Long Live!" rang out the voice of the party spokesperson. The stadium roared in affirmative unison.

"Greetings, you mighty people!" roared Mr Whiper, raising his right hand in salute. He was known to be a charismatic orator. He had his audience in a trance of some sort. Listeners ate out of his hand. He seemed to know almost everything. Mr Whiper owned eleven large farms on the outskirts of the city. He produced almost all farm products such as milk, maize, vegetables, fruits, poultry, meat, wool, wine, ostrich feathers, sunflower and hay. He employed a number of casual and permanent labourers. His permanent workers were tenants on his properties. They were made to pay rent for residing on his farms. They enjoyed certain liberties in return for keeping their limited livestock, cultivation of small fields and a cemetery. He boasted that he was liberal and afforded his labour force basic rights. He had a mud structure on each of his farms which was used as a school and a church alternatively. He inherited the farms from his grandparents. Four farms were from his maternal side and the other seven from his paternal ancestors.

"Great people, we gathered here today to chart the way forward in respect of our God given destiny. You know that you come from great lineage. We are the descendants of intelligent and resourceful people. We civilised the world. Therefore, it is befitting to say unashamedly that the world belongs to us. Things that our people have done for the world are too numerous to mention in an occasion of this nature. It will take ages and forever to conclude. What riles me, the humble son of great people, is that there are people who do not appreciate what we have done and unashamedly bite, and bite with impunity, the hand that feeds them," Mr Whiper paused to sip a glass of water. In the meantime the audience was ecstatic.

"We literally feed them. We clothe them. We cure them. We educate them. We civilise them. Today they live in proper houses, drive motor cars on tarred roads, board trains, fly aeroplanes, know about the internet, listen to the radio and watch TV. They can use cell phones and computers. We freed them from the grip of their witchdoctors and introduced decent medication and built hospitals for them. What do they say in return? 'Whites are racist and do not belong here.' Will they ever survive without us? The answer is a big NO!" he said emphatically to a tumultuous cheer.

"We have to put them back into their cages, caves and holes. We are in control of big companies such as banks, factories, mines, and various institutions. We created all these things ourselves. Now they want to take over our creations. Why can't they come up with their own? Guess what, they lack creative genes. We have a solution though. Let us keep them indebted. Ensnare them in debt traps. Don't worry about them when they are addicted to gambling, booze and drugs. That way they won't bother us. They will know who the boss is," he paused to acknowledge the applause.

"Yes, placate only those who are influential to keep the masses in check. Comply with their sorry laws by fronting their own. Promote, in the media, only those who are friendly and deny the radical ones any platform to inspire their people to be rebellious. Demonise the irresponsible revolutionary demagogues. Who do they think they are to challenge the master? Deny them heroes of their own. Make sure that their history is written by us or the moderate ones. These people are easily swayed. Besides, they are not prudent enough to fathom propaganda. Make them aspire to be like us but make sure they never attain the status. Keep it as a pipe dream. You must make them want to speak, live and dress like us. Make them crave our food. Yes, we can do all that since we are in control of the media. Portray them as subhuman or imprudent and performers of odd jobs in advertisements. They will not notice that," he paused to a rumbling cheer.

"I command every one of you here to go out there and fight to save our heritage. Work in your homes, at places of work, in institutions of learning and on the streets. We shall reclaim our victory," he concluded his speech to a thunderous applause and singing. There was a smile on almost everyone's face in the stadium. They were glad that God had given them a cheerful and intelligent leader.

Funkel looked at his father who seemed to savour every moment of the occasion. He was surprised. How so many people fell for that man's delusional utterances was beyond his comprehension. He realised that a lot still had to be done if peace and freedom for all was to be achieved. He knew that there were thousands of people who felt like him. Those people had to be brought into the open to counteract that conservative trend. He vowed not to be derailed from the cause of justice and equal rights.

Funkel was very quiet on the road back home. His father tried to whip up conversation but to no avail. Piet assumed that he was exhausted. When they arrived at home and were sitting in the lounge for refreshments, his mother asked his father how it was at the meeting.

"It was great. You should have been there. Mr Whiper was as magnificent as always. I thank God for giving us such an inspirational leader like him. He is so intelligent. If after today there is any white person who still doubts the might of our race, woe betide him or her!" said Piet, showing content in what he heard said by his leader. Funkel shrugged his shoulders as a sign of disapproval. He knew that his father was referring to him.

"I hope you will not disappoint me, my son. I want you to defend your heritage against the hyenas that are intent upon reaping where they had never sown. It is incumbent upon you as the youth to take the baton and continue with the race for the sake of your children's children," said Piet, taking a gulp of foamy beer from a bottle.

"You know my views in respect of that, Dad. I believe in one nation and diverse cultures. That is the rainbow nation, where equality and peace reign," Funkel said defiantly.

"You must remember that your fathers have your best interests at heart, Funkel," said Debora, showing concern that her son seemed not interested in preservation of White hegemony and Euro-centrism.

"Mom, I have never heard such cynical speech in my life. We live in a fast paced global village. It is not the age of *ossewa* and canon fire. You must accept that things have changed. We need to live together in harmony as different racial groups. Separate development has done damage to many old people who share your outmoded views," said Funkel. Debora's heart nearly stopped when she heard her son, the heir to the estate, express pro- Black sentiment. She had a gut feeling that her son would jettison his white values and norms.

"You cannot go against the grain my boy. God made us different for a reason. If we promote racial integrity we will be defying His will. Who are we to question what He created?" said Debora.

"Mom, God made everyman equal. We are the same people. Haven't you heard of the *Cradle of Mankind*?" he asked, hoping to ram sense into his conservative parents.

"That is rubbish. My superior people originated in the North. I will not accept the ill-conceived theory that we have common origin with blacks," added Piet, shaking his head and slamming his fist on the coffee table.

"That was scientifically proven Dad. Remember that particular discovery was made by a white professor, one of your own Dad," argued Funkel.

"Some whites are weak enough to fall for the tricks of the savages. They need to be exorcised of that evil spirit," said Piet.

"Your racism is implacable. It will take a miracle to make you see reason," said Funkel.

"Watch your tongue young man!" exclaimed Debora, pointing a finger at her son. Funkel chuckled, stood up and ran upstairs to prepare himself for bed. He still had a long trip back to university the following day. Piet and Debora remained in the lounge for a while chatting about their personal issues until they decided to retire to bed.

While chatting in their bedroom the issue of a right daughter- in-law for their son came up. "This boy needs to be led to the right girl, honey. I am afraid if we let him make his own choice he will disappoint us. His outspoken liberalism will definitely cloud his choice," said Piet.

"It is only a fleeting whim. He will soon come to his senses when he realises that he has so much to lose if he continues to advocate black ideology," said Debora, yawning to show that it was time to fall asleep. Piet remained wide awake for a while. His mind was filled with questions about his son. He was beginning to blame himself for sending his son to boarding school and not spending much time with him to instil the right values in him. He could afford the best private school in the city since he had the means. If only he had taken him to ordinary white school he would perhaps be holding a different outlook on life. He thought it wasn't too late to mend.

6

There was a furore at the Laager University over interracial student relationships. Different student organisations were preparing for the coming Student Representative Council elections. Racial integration, gender equity, academic terrorism and university fees were the main bones of contention in canvassing for the votes.

Nogana was nominated to organise election campaign for the Revolutionary Democratic Youth Movement (REDYM). The REDYM wanted to win white members of the student body by charting a non-racial and non-sexist progressive election manifesto. Nogana as Chief Strategist saw the relationship between Mpho and Funkel as an impetus for launching her campaign. She recruited Mpho and Funkel to join the REDYM and were immediately appointed as coordinators. They were given t- shirts bearing the logo of REDYM.

There were other student movements that were on the far left and far right which were involved in the campaign for SRC elections as well. The Socialist Democratic Movement (SDM) pursued radical socialist ideology with Afrocentric leanings. The Folks Party Youth (FPY) advocated exclusive white conservatism. They clung to white supremacy and separatism. The

REDYM was regarded as moderate compared to the two.

The *Night of Long Debate* was organised by the administration of Laager University. It took place in the Main Hall. All election candidates were given the opportunity to garner support from the student body by baring their personal convictions and election manifestos. Students were also afforded chance to ask their prospective leaders pertinent questions. The FPY representatives were the first to announce their manifesto. They were represented by Jaas and Jerome. Jerome as the spokesperson was the first to speak:

"Good evening ladies and gentlemen. I am here to speak on behalf of FPY. As you know this is the student organisation that had ruled Laager University for a long time in the past, almost since the creation of this institution by our forefathers," there were jeers and applause from opponents and supporters respectively.

"I state irrefutable facts only. Our FPY is synonymous with the success and quality that this institution is famous for. We have seen a deterioration of standards since the inception of current regime of leadership at our University. This is compounded by lack of will on the part of the management to ward off intruding disruptive elements masquerading as children of democracy," there was a commotion that nearly disrupted the meeting. Intervention by the Dean of Students calmed the unruly students and Jerome was allowed to continue:

"Fellow students we do not have to bury our heads in the sand about these matters. We know and everybody can see that standards have drastically dropped. We are here to obtain qualifications towards our chosen careers. We need to be seen as a mark of high quality as this institution has always been. If we are elected we shall make sure that this institution reclaims its glorious eminence. First we will make sure that admission to this University is based on merit. It should be a no-go terrain for lazy and arrogant so-called formerly disadvantaged students. They still hide behind this lame excuse even when they have been in government for decades. What a shame! These are the ones who are responsible for deterioration. Lecturers should not lower standards to accommodate them. Bad payers who are wont to be disruptive should go to institutions that they can afford.

It is nobody's fault if they cannot afford. They should learn to live within their means other than aspire for what is beyond their reach," said Jerome amidst jeers and applause. He returned to his seat with his head held high and walking in defiant gait.

Next was the popular REDYM that took the platform. It was represented by Nogana and Funkel. When the name of Nogana was called the hall erupted in song and dance. The din went on for a while and Nogana raised her clenched fist as a sign of acknowledgement and call for calm.

"Comrades, revolutionary greetings!" she shouted, "Viva REDYM, Viva!" the hall replied with a rapture. "I stand before you as your humble servant, not as a spoilt *klein baas,*" the hall chuckled and whistled in amusement.

"Comrades, it is heart breaking to realise that we still have young people who are not fast paced enough to be abreast of modern times. These archaic misfits need to be awakened from their nightmare before it is too late," said Nogana and the hall burst in laughter. "My God said forgive them because they don't know what they are doing," said Nogana and the hall hollered *Hallelujah.*

"Let me, without further ado get to the business of the evening. You all know that REDYM is a progressive student organisation. We represent peace and freedom. If you vote for us you vote for equality and better education for all. We subscribe to human rights for all irrespective of race, creed, gender and financial status. We believe that all of us here deserve to live in peace and harmony. Discrimination is a swear word to us. We are here to undo the injustices of the past for the sake of national reconciliation. You, as young people, are going to take over the administration of this country in the near future. It is here where you should be afforded the opportunity to learn to become real human beings. You should be allowed to shed sadist racism, tribalism and sexism. All who deserve to be educated should be afforded that opportunity to attain their qualifications. None of us should be excluded on the basis of affordability of the fees. We will make sure that our institution, the government and the corporate world offer bursaries to enable our brothers and sisters, Black, Coloured, Indian and White to complete their studies. We would also like the management to introduce mixed hostels. If we are able to mix in the classes, halls, libraries and places of worship why is it a taboo to have mixed hostels? It is time the management showed trust in us. We are responsible law abiding citizens of this country," concluded Nogana. She led a revolutionary song and the hall erupted into a deafening chant, *Nogana my President*. It took the Programme Director almost ten minutes to steer the audience back to course.

The next to speak was the representative of the SDM. It was represented by a hefty boy nicknamed Trotsky and a lanky, burly looking Sempue. Trotsky was a handsome looking young man who was light in complexion. He was popular with girls because of his model features. He was also a good Hip-Hop singer celebrated on campus. There was an encouragement from a handful of supporters gathered at the left corner of the hall. Their symbolic song lacked the impact of the previous one. The previous speakers seemed a hard act to follow. He held a microphone in his hand and moved towards the edge of the stage. He only had a small piece of paper in his hand:

"Comrades, compatriots and aliens," he said with fierce grin on his face. There was a murmur and acknowledgement from a few supporters.

"I know some of you are wondering why I include aliens in my greetings. Fellow students we have aliens wedged in our midst. These are those who have no interest of Africa and its indigenous people at heart. They are the people who still view Africa and everything about it as dark and backward. I am talking about those who still clandestinely subscribe to the misguided philosophy of Social Darwinism. These are the ones who still pursue the policy of exclusivity calculated to keep the poor at bay as regards access to education. These people are not necessarily classified in terms of colour. I wouldn't say they are white since we do have naive black brothers and sisters who acquiesce to alien discriminatory agenda.

Comrades, it is surprising to hear a person who purports to represent the poor still putting a capitalist price to education. They talk about loans and bursaries for poor students. But how many young and old poor brothers and sisters are out there in the cold without that financial assistance they make so much noise about? There are hundreds of thousands, if not millions of intelligent students who failed to get those bursaries, comrades. Yes, the few that manage to get the loan remain highly indebted because they still have to repay the loan amount plus interest. The discount they so much harp about is nothing but tokenism. Many of our fellow students who find it hard to get employment straight from college or university are 'black listed'. When they enter the labour market their good names are already tarnished in the name of education for the poor. Comrades, if the master eats all the meat and thereafter throws the bones at you, do not lick or gnaw at them. You must throw them back at him or else he might think that you appreciate the insult. Don't afford him a clean conscience. We as SRM say that education should be free from pre-school to the first degree. If we are elected, we will lobby the management of this institution in particular, to scrap the fees," he was interrupted by whistling and ululations.

"It is the strategy of our former oppressors to prolong subtle exclusion through exorbitant fees. Remember that these people pillaged our natural resources and exploited our fathers to enrich themselves. They still command economic advantage and lead life of affluence at our expense. Their ploy is to make things they deem crucial to their usurped status inaccessible to the majority of us. They create lapdog lieutenants in the form of new elite who speak the language of the poor and tell you what you want to hear in polished English. It is all a facade. This way they maintain their bigoted supremacy. It is sad to realise that there are brothers and sisters who have been co-opted as pawns in this game. Yes, it is true that we have our own that still give these people esteem boast by hankering after Eurocentric features and culture. These sell-outs are prepared to be used in window dressing this farcical freedom. Remember there is no slave master who will allow his slave to attain equal status and freedom. These lost sheep need to be found and brought back to the flock. They cannot be left in the care of the leopards who continue to devour them and use their skins to deceive us. SRM is the only genuine student organisation that can lift the veil from the eyes of the naïve false prophets who shout from the roof tops claiming to be the voice of the poor when indeed they perpetuate white hegemony. They have their fat fingers-tips in the honey and think they have truly attained freedom. Singing people's songs and dancing to the African beat does not mean they are genuine. Don't be fooled by their big bellies or cars and think it means freedom. It is nothing but a symbol of greed. I have seen some of these cheats boast about their material possessions. Are they true revolutionaries? No they are wolves in sheep skins.

Comrades we have noticed with grave concern that the lecturing staffs of this institution are tainted by a few elements that have a tendency to play a 'god' with the careers of African students. These sadists should not be allowed to flourish on our campus. They victimise our poor fellow students to further their own twisted egos. There are members of the student body who abet this malady afflicting us by pandering to the whims of these psychotic and arrogant lecturers. SRM is the only organisation that has the right policy and passionate crew that can rid this institution of these academic terrorists masquerading as intelligent professors. They are not here to help Africa but to stunt our development. We will not allow any lecturer to terrorise any student on campus. They are here because we are here. Our parents spend hard earned money to see us through university. We will not allow these academic predators to maul our future. Do not be fooled by the timid REDYM and delusional FPY. They will only perpetuate your suffering. Vote for freedom and fairness! Vote SRM! Viva SRM viva!" he shouted, raised his clenched fist and went back to his sit. He seemed to have added a few supporters to his organisation since he got a standing ovation.

Jaas was disturbed by the support shown to REDYM and SRM. He mused that his heritage was in danger of being submerged by invasion from the descendants of his fathers' servants. He blamed himself and all white people who seemed to be doing nothing to defeat those leaning towards racial integration. He blamed those missionaries who first taught Africans the education that freed them from ignorance. "Why didn't the whites who first came here leave blacks in their backward state? Now they think they understand democracy and the ways of life of white people. They are taking over from us," he quietly pondered, oblivious to the proceedings in the hall. He was awakened by a jostle from Jerome who asked him if he wanted to answer the question posed by one student in the audience. He jerked and Jerome realised that he was not concentrating. "What was the question?" asked Jaas, a little embarrassed. The audience noticed that and hollered in laughter. "The student wanted to know if you would share a room with a black student," said Jerome. Jaas stood up to answer the question. He was booed by the audience but stood his ground.

"Do not get me wrong. I am not racist. All I believe in is peace between different people and the only way to achieve this is if we respect one another's space. Good fences make good neighbours. A room is too intimate for me so I would rather share it with someone a little identical," said Jaas, cementing his racial conviction. There was a comical laughter in the audience.

Another student wanted to know from REDYM what notion their mixed-gender hostels policy was based on. Funkel was the one who stood up to answer the question. He was acknowledged with a deafening applause.

"We in the REDYM do not judge people in terms of their outward physical appearance, religion and gender but quality of their inner selves. We believe that the sharing of rooms between members of different racial background will engender national reconciliation, integration and peace. We tend to fear the unknown. We fear those who are different from us. *Apartheid* denied our people that knowledge and experience hence our reluctance. Let us not condemn the ignorant but help them see reason so they will come on board and help to build this nation. The likes of Jaas are still stuck in the past. They need to be persistently shown that their nostalgia is insignificant and unrealistic. As regards mixed hostels we base our demand on the fact that people should live together in harmony irrespective of their gender. We believe that separate gender hostels promote sexism. We don't call for sharing of rooms by males and females though because that would be a recipe for disaster. We would prefer female blocks of residences within formerly exclusive male areas and vice versa," said Funkel. He was given a standing ovation for his smart utterances.

Nogana was elated to have found a perfect leverage in Funkel.

Her critics were now praising her for her foresightedness.

He would help woe moderate white students and those who doubted REDYM's policy of non-racialism and non-sexism.

Jaas and the leadership of FPY came out of the meeting scalded and prostrate. They vowed to resuscitate their prowess by attacking their critics from their weakest point. They sat in Jaas's room and strategized. Jerome was their chief tactician.

"Guys, if we are worth our salt we should not surrender to the enemy. We have lost a battle not a war," he suggested, taking a deep sucking at his cigarette. He gave off a long puff. The room was full of smoke despite a widely opened window.

"We firstly have to neutralise Funkel who has deserted to the enemy. He is providing mileage to REDYM. We have to win these elections at all costs. Friend or no friend, when we are done with Funkel we pounce on the top brass of both REDYM and SRM. Every sensible white person heard the corrosive anti-white diatribe delivered by SRM. Every chain has a weak point however strong it may seem. I have an idea of how to infiltrate them," said Jaas, showing confidence.

Meanwhile SRM was also frightened by REDYM's seemingly overwhelming support that they commanded and contrived a way of neutralising them. It would not be a walk in the park as it appeared. Their mainstay of attack would be the discrediting of its members as hypocrites who pretended to love the poor but pursued the aspirations of the new capitalist elite.

The REDYM was intent on entrenching their hold and expanding their support base through their progressive policy. As the ruling student organisation, they had access to the resources of the university which they channelled into their campaign. They also had enough funding from their mother body party and the corporate world that saw them as moderate enough to be promoted. They were able to organise their own meetings, print T-shirts, pamphlets and prize competitions. They dominated the campus radio station and developed their own website. They acquired contact details of the students and reached them through SMS's, Twitter and other social networks. They used youth structures in churches, cultural and sports clubs. Their campaign was well organised.

7

One late Saturday afternoon Funkel and Mpho were walking hand in hand returning from a nearby off campus park when they were attacked by a group of people wearing balaclavas. Mpho sustained minor injuries but was emotionally traumatised. Funkel was the one who was severely injured. They were both hospitalised. Funkel sustained broken ribs, a fractured arm and bruises all over the face. He stayed in hospital for almost two weeks. The attack smacked of political motive since nothing was taken from the victims.

Funkel's parents quickly flew to the hospital when they heard what had befallen their son. They found him in excruciating pain and bandaged. His mom shed tears as she could not bear to see her son in that state. Piet uttered obscene words cursing the rogues who did that to his son and blamed the police for their laxity. He used racial slur in lambasting the incumbent government.

"Incompetent numskulls!" he said, feeling his blood boiling. "They have allowed marauding criminals latitude to do as they please. If this country was still ruled by whites this nonsense would not be happening," said Piet with a hiss. Funkel told him that they didn't see the attackers' faces so they were unidentifiable. What made Piet angrier was the fact that his son was in the company of a black girl when the incident happened. That made his demon of hatred to fill him with all sorts of malicious intent. He could not contain his anger. He gasped for air as he struggled to breathe. He paused to regain his power to talk.

"I told you to stay away from that girl. Those people are nothing but trouble. Was she injured as well?" asked Piet. "Yes, luckily she sustained only minor injuries," said Funkel, with a mild cough.

"You say luckily. Don't you see? This girl planned the whole thing. She must be arrested," said Anna, sobbing and wiping tears from her eyes.

"No, it is only your imagination. Mpho loves me. She cannot do such a horrible thing to me. This smacks of perverts who are against our relationship," said Funkel.

"You must have been bewitched by this girl," said his mother. "Mom you are a Christian. How could you judge a child of God so harshly?" asked Funkel, disturbed by where that conversation was leading. Funkel was reluctant to relent to accusations of this heinous act levelled against the love of his life.

"Those people do not know God. White people tried hard to make them relinquish their worship of the witchdoctor without success. Even the few who are converted still regress to their demonic ways during trying times. So don't ever call any of them a child of God," said Piet.

"I am extremely disappointed. I sometimes wish I didn't know you. It is just that one cannot choose parents," said Funkel looking exceedingly dejected.

Meanwhile Mpho walked into the room where Funkel was, unaware that he had visitors. Altercation ensued as Funkel's parents admonished Mpho. They told her in no uncertain terms to stay away from their son. Mpho was taken by surprise because she thought Funkel's parents were as civil as their son. She noticed a stark contrast. She scurried out of the room holding her mouth and fighting back tears. She collided with a group of people in the corridor. It was Jaas and his entourage paying Funkel a visit. They didn't apologise but only shoved her aside and passed on looking menacingly at her. She felt a shiver down her spine and her gut told her that there was something sinister about them. "This bunch of numskulls who think people should worship the ground they walk on," she thought, "they always seem to transgress with impunity," she mumbled to herself. She hurried down the hallway eager to get out of that place as quickly as possible.

Meanwhile in Funkel's room a symposium was held by the legion of white supremacy. Funkel's father was in rapport with his son's friends. He saw in them the heirs to the mantle of white hegemony and values. If only his son was fretful about preservation of white identity like those young vanguards, his dream would be fulfilled. He judged himself as a failed parent. What had the parents of those brave young men done well that he so dismally failed to achieve? He wondered.

"Young men, you must hammer sense into this boy's head. He seems possessed. He doesn't appreciate what we, your fathers and our forebears have done for the world. You have to take the baton and continue the stride to eternal supremacy. You will only abandon that just course at your own peril," said Piet, with stern gaze on his face. Jaas was licking the honey that came out of the old man's mouth.

"My friend Funkel frolics with the enemy. He has let down his guard. He is caught in the morass of the devil's trap. We tried to warn him but he chose to turn a deaf ear. Look what they have done to him. Damn scoundrels!" exclaimed Jaas.

"You seem to have full knowledge of who is responsible for this dastardly deed. Maybe you will give the police the information that they require to arrest the culprits," retorted Funkel. Jaas nearly choked with fear. He jerked when he heard the mention of police interrogation.

"It is obvious who did this to you. Probably, your girlfriend's jealous boyfriend hired them. These people have no morals. They sleep around," said Jerome.

"You stop right there Jerome," interjected Funkel, "I cannot allow you to bad mouth innocent people. Anyone could have done this. Even you all do have a motive. I should report you as primary suspects in this matter," said Funkel, wriggling in pain.

"How can we attack our own friend? We must avenge your assault. They cannot get away with this. We will find them. I promise you," said Jaas.

"Who are they?" asked Funkel.

"Stop being a hot head, Funkel!" rejoined Debora.

"Please listen to what these brave young men are saying. They have your best interest at heart," said Piet.

"Thanks a lot for your interest. I don't want anyone starting a war on my account. I am a peace loving person. I know you want to go out smashing the heads of innocent people in the name of vengeance. I know you have always wanted an excuse to start a racial fight. That is not going to solve any problem. What it will definitely achieve will be more suffering and hatred. That is the last thing I would like to see, especially when I am the cause. The police will do their job. Do not take the law in your own hands, please!" pleaded Funkel.

"The police are corrupt. How on earth do you hope for anything positive in this rotten country? Open your eyes and stop dreaming. No police cares about your interest. They are all incompetent just like their government," snapped Piet.

"We don't want to lose you, my son," said Debora, "please listen to us. We have been around for a while. Why would you trust people who are different from you and turn your back on your own?" she asked.

Trying to convince Funkel to change his mind seemed like watering a stone. Their hostile missiles only served to solidify his attitude. He was of a different mould.

"Mom, I judge a person guilty on the basis of concrete evidence. Your utterances make all of you capable of inhuman act of violence fanned by racial hatred. On the contrary I have not heard any of those people that you hasten to accuse say bad things about white people. What you say is what you are," retorted Funkel.

"Who do you think you are? A white Mandela or Martin Luther Jr?" asked Jaas.

"I know who I am. I am Funkel. One who is intent on pursuing peace and justice for all," replied Funkel.

There was disappointment on the faces of all who gathered there. Funkel's non-racialism seemed like a hard nut to crack. His parents were convinced that he needed exorcism.

Jaas, together with his entourage, vowed to fix the arrogant blacks and left the room. Funkel and his parents remained to conclude their discussion.

Mpho met Nogana, who was in the company of several students, outside the male hospital ward. They were on their way to pay them a visit. She narrated her ordeal to them and they were taken aback. They thought Funkel came from a liberal white family given his progressive views.

They knew the kind of welcome awaiting them when they arrived at Funkel's room, thanks to Mpho's tips. They sharpened their mouth swords and poised their wits' shields to ward off imminent assault. Piet was enraged by the sight of those he regarded as aliens.

"So, you have come to marvel at your masterpiece, huh? There, take a good look. You have done a good job," snapped Piet. Nogana calmly ignored the old man's accusation.

"Good afternoon, Sir. You must be Funkel's father. How do you do?" said Nogana stretching out her hand towards Piet. Piet turned aside and looked away.

"I don't shake hands with the likes of you. What are you doing here anyway? You are not family. Only family members are supposed to be here. Please, get out," said Piet pointing his fat finger towards the open door.

"It is fine Dad. They are my friends," said Funkel, gesticulating that they come in.

"My child these people are not worth your soiled socks. How can you debase yourself like this?" said Piet.

"Mr Koekemoer, with all due respect, you have no right to insult us like that. If it wasn't for Funkel I would return the favour," said Nogana.

"Hi, Guys. I am happy that you came. One needs sunshine after a gloomy night, hey? By the way, how is the campaign going? We must win these elections at all costs," said Funkel.

"All we need is your input. Get well soon so we can work for democratic victory. This nefarious act should only make you steadfast. Let's soldier on comrade," said Nogana raising her revolutionary fist. Piet hollered for security to come and drag those exasperating youths out of his son's room. The group realised how precarious the situation was and quickly vacated the room.

Piet was fuming and he reprimanded his son for the shame he brought their respected family. "I have every reason to disown you now!" exclaimed Piet. Funkel lay quiet for a while and only stared at the ceiling while his father continued with his reproach. He lay there like a hapless sheep being shorn. He wanted to tell his father to get lost but baulked despite that being so irresistibly tantalising. Piet paced round the room. He kicked and punched the wall several times. Every time he assailed the inanimate wall his wife would flinch. When time for the visit elapsed, Piet dragged his wife out of the room without saying goodbye to his son. Debora was looking back with her mouth half open intending to utter a word to her son but failed. Tears were rolling down her eyes. That was the picture Funkel wished to forget quickly.

Meanwhile on campus, the Laager Campus Radio was broadcasting election debate where candidates elaborated on their election manifestos in an attempt to woe voters. It was a racially charged debate. One caller wanted to know why FPY were advocating outmoded views and what good their segregationist policy would do for national reconciliation. Jerome as the representative of FPY was emphatic. "What we propagate is maintenance of standards set out by descendants of Europeans who settled in and civilised the backward nations found inhabiting this part of the world. We are the custodians of those values and norms," said Jerome.

"Jerome, do you insinuate that your counterparts are anti-development and will steer this institution into the rocks if they were to be voted back into power?" asked host DJ Prime. Calling oneself by those queer names was in vogue. Every nonentity coined a fancy name for themselves in an attempt to break into the clustered entertainment industry.

REDYM's representative, Nogana interjected, "Reactionary elements like FPY tread on thin ice. Their outmoded ideas fern racial hate. This could ignite civil war in this volatile country of ours. Progressive minded organisations like REDYM work for national reconciliation and peace. Our membership represents the demographics of this country. Voting REDYM means everybody will enjoy equal opportunities. Jerome and his like-minded are only suffering from twisted nostalgia. We shall never ever go back there. This country is free and ruled by democratic leaders. We want to see that in our institutions of learning which represent the larger society out there. As leaders of tomorrow we need to sow the seeds of peace and democracy," Nogana quipped.

Trotsky of SDM cut in, "SDM stands for the rights of the marginalised. These are the victims of colonial exclusion and exploitation. REDYM talk about equal opportunities for all. We say you cannot talk of equal opportunities until the playing field has been levelled. You cannot pit the disadvantaged against the privileged. The playing field at the moment is so uneven that the disadvantaged are clandestinely set to fail. We say, as SDM, that Africans should be placed a hundred paces ahead to enable them to win the race since they are running barefoot. REDYM is overly obsessed with the so called reconciliation at the expense of ignorant masses. Whites will always hold tenaciously to their privileges. They will never ever surrender the edge they have unless it is wrestled from them. So REDYM should stop burying their heads in the sand and face reality. Whites will never change or allow Africans to be their equals. All they are interested in is maintenance of the status quo that favours them. They will support the moderate who unwittingly prop up white hegemony. I mean the likes of REDYM."

Jerome butted in, "You talk about whites as if they are not truly African. However, they have every right to have the edge. It is a God given position, besides we worked hard for all the things we now have. Stop your racist jealousy and envy."

"Worked hard?" Trotsky interposed, "worked hard my foot! The only time a white person works hard is when he fathoms how to deprive and deprave weaker nations," he said.

"No, no, no," said Jerome, with his face pale red with anger, "we civilised the world," retorted Jerome.

"Yeah, that is right. You wiped some American Indian tribes, the aborigines in South East Asia, plundered resources in Latin America, Africa, Asia and the Middle East, just to mention a few. That is the blood trail of your civilisation. You destroyed indigenous institutions, values, norms and languages because you felt they threatened your colonial imposition and usurpation," said Trotsky.

One caller raised a concern about lecturers who deliberately taught in the medium of Afrikaans which was foreign to many students.

Jerome stated, "Those lecturers have a right to lecture in the language they best understand and are comfortable with. It is a pity that a few blacks do not understand the language. We appreciate their concern but they are the ones who came to this

University where lecturers happen to be Afrikaans speakers. They should learn to cope or leave."

Nogana intervened, "We take serious exception to lecturers who exercise subtle exclusion through language that is not understood by black students. How do they expect these poor students to pass their courses if they are disadvantaged? The interests of the students should be paramount. We call upon those lecturers to reform or retire."

Trotsky cut in, "I don't understand why these racists continue to live in Africa if they loathe Africans this way. Africans have sustained their European economies for ages. We provide resources for their secondary industries and markets for their commercial products. How do they repay us? A parasite will never nurse a host. The clock is ticking though. Africans are now wiser. Once bitten twice shy. It is in their own interest that they should change."

"Blacks are the ones who are provocative. Now as we speak my friend Funkel is lying in hospital after being attacked. How are we supposed to be peaceful when we live in a hostile environment?" asked Jerome.

"You can't say for a fact that Funkel was attacked by blacks. Criminal activities know no colour. Funkel is our best friend and an active member of REDYM. We will only know those responsible when they are apprehended and convicted in a court of law. Until then let us desist from wild accusations. They are malicious," Nogana rejoined.

One caller asked them to contrast what everybody would lose if racial fighting ensued and also what they stood to gain in national reconciliation or compromise. Gains seemed to outweigh losses. All agreed that war was not in the best interest of anyone as it entailed grim consequences. Uneasy truce was reached.

8

Mpho was discharged. She headed home where she would rest and recuperate fully. Her parents were rattled by that incident. They couldn't bear to lose their only child. They thanked God for saving their child from harm's grip. Rampho felt like taking a trip down to the scene of the attack and search for the attackers himself. He vowed to wring their wretched necks if he came across them. He was glad though that she was not badly hurt.

"Tell me about the incident. You haven't really told us the details of the attack,' said Rampho. Mpho didn't know where to start. She was so traumatised that talking about it would trigger a relapse.

"We were taken by surprise. These rascals pounced on us from nowhere. I was with Funkel chatting and having fun when out of the blue the disguised five-some launched their blitz. We least expected it as they attacked from behind. It happened so fast we couldn't fight back. Besides they would still overpower us as they were armed. We screamed for help and when people came to our rescue after hearing our cries, they had already fled the scene," said Mpho, pausing to catch her breath.

"Did you see or hear anything that can help identify them?" asked Rampho. Mpho paused as if trying to recall any valuable evidence. Her mind went blank.

"Who is this Funkel boy you were with? Is he your boyfriend or what?" asked Rampho, staring his daughter in the eyes. Mpho almost fainted. She froze for a while. She looked at her mother hoping she would come to her rescue. Mampho was indifferent. She seemed to be tacitly saying to her that it was none of her own business.

"Mpho, did you hear me?" asked Rampho, determined to hear the answer.

"We are only friends Dad," said Mpho sheepishly. Rampho could see that his daughter was keeping something from him.

"Is he perhaps not the one who brought this unto you or his jealous girlfriend trying to get back at him?" asked Rampho, "I don't like this idea of you dating boys at university. We sent you there to study not to fool around," said the old man. Mampho sensed desperation in her daughter.

"Papa you know that Mpho is a good girl. She knows what she wants," interjected Mampho.

"I hope that does not include boys," said Rampho.

"Even if it did, Mpho is a grown up. She is responsible," said Mampho.

"Hold it right there! She will only be a grown up when she has graduated. Until then she is still a little girl to me," said Rampho.

"Don't worry Dad. I am careful. I wouldn't jeopardise my education for anything. I am determined to achieve my goals," said Mpho.

Rampho contemplated the idea of going out to consult as he suspected witchcraft or ancestral antagonism in all that happened. He set out on a trip to a secluded village in the Drakensberg Mountains. There lived a famed ferocious traditional doctor whose mystical bones never lied. He had consulted with him on several occasions and he never disappointed. He felt it befitting to seek professional opinion on that occasion. As a traditionalist he felt it was incumbent upon him not to expose his family to man-made dangers. His own father once told him that, 'a real man does not let his family live under a Marula tree. A man has to buttress.'

On arrival he was met by three trainee *sangomas* who ordered him to take off his shoes. He was led through a long zigzagging passage that ascended to Diabolela's hut. He found the great *sangoma* awaiting him. He roared, belched and trembled hysterically and Rampho's hair stood on edge. There was an eerie feeling about the place. It felt like he was on a different planet. He came to this place several times but he never got used to it. It seemed a new place every time.

"I have been expecting you," said Diabolela, roaring like a lion caught in a hunter's trap. "*Makhosi!*" replied Rampho, acknowledging the *sangoma's* allegation. One doesn't question the authority of a *sangoma* lest you are seen as being disrespectful. Rampho was asked to pay a consultation fee which he did without rancour. He was asked to blow into the bones pouch for diagnosis to begin. The pouch was emptied onto a reed mat. Bones and shells were scattered all over. Diabolela stared at the mystical paraphernalia and murmured inexplicable words.

Rampho was anxious to hear the verdict. His heart was pounding like a bass drum. The sound felt so loud that he thought the *sangoma* could hear it.

"My child, these bones are troubled," he said, pinching his snuff and sprinkling it upon the bones. He took a deep sniff of the snuff, shrugged, trembled and gave a fierce roar. He ordered Rampho to pick up the bones once again. He said a few words and ordered Rampho to repeat after him. He told him to throw the bones onto the mat. He whistled, shook his head and snarled. Rampho had reason to be more afraid. He waited for the sage's diagnosis.

"My child, I see a dark cloud hanging over your head. This entails trouble. Your ancestors are not happy. Your great grandfather's aunt wants you to slaughter a beast for her. She says you have not named your daughter after her. If you do not do that she will bring bad luck to you and your family," said Diabolela, "*vumani bo!*" exclaimed the great *sangoma*. "Siya vuma!" hollered Rampho in acknowledgement. He gave him herbs and liquid medicine to chase away evil spirits and ward off witches. He said he should administer the herbs to his daughter and make all in the family drink some. He picked up the package and left without saying goodbye. It is said that you do not thank a traditional doctor or say goodbyes because that might render the medicine useless.

On his way back home Rampho was pondering on how he was going to convince his family to take the doctor's prescription as they purported they were averse to traditional stuff. Mampho is a devoted member of an orthodox church while his daughter is a born again Christian. Although Rampho is a church-goer, he doubles up as a traditionalist. He straddles both worlds as it is a norm in modern society.

Convincing the two to comply would be a steep hill to climb. His wife ranted and raved when she discovered her husband's jaunt.

"You will not go anywhere near my child with that evil stuff of yours. We are Christians for heaven's sake!" exclaimed Mampho. Rampho felt like his authority as the head of the family was slipping through his fingers.

"You'll do as I say, woman!" screamed Rampho, banging his fist on the table, "as the head of this house I cannot afford to place the life of my child in danger. I'll do what my ancestors used to do before Westerners came and scuppered their way of life. ," he said.

Mampho was so angry that she staged a walk out. Rampho ordered her to sit down. She turned and looked at him with a frown. Rampho could read contempt in his wife's eyes. He thought how different it would have been if he had married Mabotse whom he ditched after meeting Mampho. Mabotse was different because she was not very educated. She never questioned Rampho. He regretted his foolishness.

"What happened to you my husband? You are a church elder. What will the priest say if he finds out about what you have done?" asked Mampho.

"Are you going to tell everybody in church your family secrets?" asked Rampho.

"My priest is not everybody. I cannot hide anything from my priest," said Mampho.

"Priests are human beings my wife. They are not God. They have their own weaknesses. They run around under cover of the night to consult the same *sangomas*. They in turn tell you not to go to these people. What a hypocrisy!" said Rampho.

"You know what you are saying isn't true. They are the ones who teach us that ours is a jealous God. He doesn't want to share His people with earthly gods," retorted Mampho.

"Believe what you like. Only if a moonless night could suddenly turn into a clear day. You would be surprised who the devil is," Rampho replied.

Mampho swore on her mother's grave that the *sangoma*'s herbs would not come anywhere near herself or her daughter. When reason failed, Rampho tried to use his male coercion but without success.

He approached his daughter thinking of convincing her instead. "My girl, this world is a dangerous place. If you are not careful you could be consumed by its clandestine forces. They are lurking everywhere waiting for an opportune time to pounce on us," said

Rampho. Mpho was lost. She struggled to make sense of her father's assertion. Rampho continued, "I have been to see an old friend of mine after what happened to you at university. I wanted professional opinion on the matter as I sensed something sinister about all that," said Rampho.

"Is your friend a policeman?" asked Mpho. Rampho stared in the distance and scratched his head.

"You see my child, this man I'm talking about is known all over the world. He helped many people. Even dignitaries such as presidents seek his wisdom and powers," said Rampho.

"Is he a crime specialist?" asked Mpho.

"No. He is a specialist in his own right. He is an African traditional doctor," said Rampho, assessing his daughter's reaction.

"What? No offence Dad, you know I don't believe in those people and their scary stuff," replied Mpho.

"If you don't listen to your elders' wisdom, you will perish in the hands of your enemies. I am a church-goer myself. I was baptised. I read the Bible and know how the missionaries twisted the Word of God for their own selfish ends. There is nothing wrong with African herbs. Whites discredited the African way of life because they wanted us to be subservient to them. They could not stamp their supremacy if they allowed us to continue with our traditional norms and values. They would only be superior if they taught us their language and lifestyle. They called it civilisation as if Africans were barbaric. That was pure political strategy to mislead and subjugate us," said Rampho.

Mpho found it hard to believe what her father was saying. She had never read a book of History so she was oblivious to missionary stories, slavery and colonisation.

"Dad, aren't you being a bit too harsh on the poor white people. They are human beings like us and they have done nothing wrong. Why do some blacks hate them so much?" asked Mpho.

"There is a reason for every reaction. Blacks who hate them as you say have their reason for doing that. Who knows? They might have had a bitter experience with them. I don't think they paint them with the same brush though," said Rampho.

Mpho could still not comprehend what her father was saying. She based her reasoning on what her priest taught her about creation. He said God made man in his own image. He said that man referred to all human beings irrespective of race, gender or colour.

"Dad, the traditional doctors that you claim are so wise, why do they look so dirty and nondescript? Their medicines are kept in dirty containers notwithstanding their mucky dispensaries. I have seen them in several movies. I can't bear the sight of them," said Mpho.

"Who produced those movies?" asked Rampho.

"Come on, Dad. You know who the best movie producers are. Whites of cause!" exclaimed Mpho.

"You are utterly brainwashed my child. Don't you know that as long as whites write stories about blacks they will always portray us in a bad light. It is sheer propaganda," said Rampho. He realised the mammoth task he had to surmount in order to convince his daughter otherwise.

"You know I admire whites for their witty manipulation of human thought. If only blacks could take a leaf out of their book, we would all be free for real," Rampho quipped.

"What do you mean Dad? We are free indeed. What freedom are you talking about?" asked Mpho.

"I mean genuine freedom from playing second fiddle to whites. Freedom from aspiring to be what we are not. You know my child, my heart bleeds whenever I see a black person wearing a white person's masks and feeling content with it. I am longing to see a day where black people would be proud of their kinky hair, indigenous languages, clothes, food and beliefs. God did not create an African by mistake. Why do these Africans dishonour God by not cherishing their true being?" posed Rampho.

"Dad, we can't go back to atavism. We have long abandoned that way of life. We need to move with times. This is not the twelfth century. It is the age of the fast paced. The slow paced are out-paced and out of place" Mpho said.

"The fast paced and the lost. You have no idea how white people would be proud to hear that. You are the essence of the brainwashed," retorted Rampho.

"I am the epitome of the progressive. You on the other hand represent the slow paced who are stuck in the past. This is not the Middle Ages, Dad," said Mpho.

"Watch your tongue young woman! I am still your father you know," said Rampho, pointing his finger at Mpho.

"We are only engaged in erudite talk, Dad. Why the threats now?" joked Mpho.

"Abandoning your fathers' way of life makes you live the fast paced flimsy lifestyle that eroded your morality and reduced your life expectancy," said Rampho.

"I don't blame you for feeling that way. Every generation considers itself the best. It is human nature. I am also going to feel the same way towards my children as you feel now about us," Mpho quipped.

"When things become complicated don't say I didn't try. If my hands were not tied, I would whip you to do the right thing. Anyway, it is your life and your choice," said Rampho, feeling defeated and despondent.

Rampho stood up and went outside to catch fresh air. He stood on the veranda and cool breeze caressed his face. He took in a long deep gulp of the cool air and exhaled slowly. He fixed his eyes in the distant sky and realised it was partly cloudy. A lone eagle was circling effortlessly without flapping its wings. He marvelled at this majestic bird of prey. He envied its ability to monitor movement of its potential food on the ground and adroitness in execution of its mission. Prey would be criss-crossing on the ground, only conscious of the obvious but oblivious to eminent danger lurking far away yet so near.

He likened the scenario to a clandestine and damaging influence of propaganda. The victims are not aware of the secret hand manipulating their thinking and activities subconsciously. The youth are the target as they are still unsophisticated. What is inculcated early in life would be difficult to erase.

He was amazed at the invisible hand that controlled nature. It was awe striking to watch nature undergoing its natural balance. He realised how mankind, in pursuit of selfish ends, destabilises this natural balance. In implementation of the so-called civilisation, irreparable damage is done to the biosphere. He blamed the current global warming on man's actions.

He remembered how he saw nature at work when he visited one of large game reserves in the country. There he saw unfettered flora and fauna at its best. He appreciated the beauty of God's creation. Man was the only spoiler in this masterpiece.

He recalled that the only pitiful sight was that of a lonely lion that roamed the jungle. It had probably been ostracised by its pride on account of its age and frailness. He wondered why the members could be so forgetful that the now undesirable one had once been their pillar of strength and a strategist in the game of survival. They all trusted his prowess and protection. They followed his orders without reservation and also his craftiness in hunting. They ravenously gnawed at its tasty kills. All that meant nothing and was forgotten in the wink of an eye when it suited them. Life is not fair, he thought. You sacrifice and work your paws to the bone for the welfare of others and only to be abandoned when your services are exhausted. Those who once looked upon you for wisdom regard you as imprudent. Those who once thought you were indispensable now disposed of you like a used toilet paper. They blatantly laugh at you in your face for your foolishness.

He wondered if he was losing his grip as the head of the family. His wife and daughter had the audacity to stand up to him. They doubted his wisdom in decision making. He thought that he was to blame for that defiance since he had been too lenient and involved his wife in major decisions initially. That drifted to the norm of requiring his wife's approval in every trivial decision like buying a packet of cigarettes.

He blamed women liberation movements and government's affirmation of women's rights. He felt that it negated the norm of male dominance that was there since creation. He had qualms about constitutions. They contradicted the supreme law of the Creator, he thought. Didn't He send great prophets to this world in the male form and personality? Was that not proof that a man was created superior to a woman? He pondered. Who was he to challenge the judgement of learned men and women of law? "Who is the supreme judge, the legal experts or God?" he ruminated. He felt despondent and prostrate.

"I'll not let this woman disobey me," he vowed. He felt he was letting his ancestors down for allowing a woman dictate terms or lay rules in the family. He had to stamp his authority as the head of the family. He prepared the herbs according to the *sangoma*'s instructions. He did all that in the absence of his wife who had gone to the shops with daughter Mpho. Women love shopping, it would be ages before they returned home. He didn't want to be caught red handed though. He was afraid it would alienate his wife. He heard about several men in the township whose wives had instituted *Court Protection Order* against them and life was no bed of roses. They had become virtual prisoners in their own houses. Their expensive sofas had grown thorns. They slept in separate rooms and there was nothing they could do about it.

They married in community of property and wives knew they were entitled to half the estate of their husbands irrespective of the fact that they never worked for a salary or bought anything of value. Men were afraid of opting out of their marriages lest they forfeited their hard earned estates and custody of their children. He felt that current dispensation was harsh on men. "Didn't God make man the head at creation?" he mused.

He heard a car stopping outside. They had returned sooner. He quickly gathered his stuff, shoved them in a plastic bag and threw it into the wardrobe. Guilt was written all over his face like a child caught with a hand in a cookie jar. When Mampho arrived he asked her to sit down as he had something to tell her. "It better not be about your traditional healer," said Mampho.

"Relax, why jump to conclusions?" asked Rampho.

"I am sick and tired of your backward philosophy," snapped Mampho.

Rampho could not muster courage to speak about name change for Mpho. He realised that it was not the right time to propose it. He changed the subject to church politics. He felt that he needed to persuade his wife not to say a word to the Reverend about what transpired.

"My religion does not allow me to lie. I'll disclose your transgression the moment I find that opportunity," she said. Rampho could feel his gut moving.

"Please, don't you know that my position as the church elder will be jeopardised?" pleaded Rampho.

"You should have thought about that before you went to your *sangoma*. You didn't even bother to ask for my opinion before you left. Now you want me to be your accomplice, it won't happen!" snapped Mampho. Rampho fixed his eyes on the ground. He was speechless. There was torture and pessimism in his countenance.

He could not bear the thought of defeat. He called his older brother Ndoda and arranged that they meet at a secret place.

"*Mogale*-The Brave One!" greeted Rampho, praising his older brother.

"*Moloto*-The Preserving One!" replied Ndoda, acknowledging his younger brother's greeting with his own.

His brother did not mince his words. He accused his younger brother of being a weakling as a result of a love potion that was seemingly administered by his wife. He suggested that he put his wife in line. He suggested that he had to mete out stern treatment.

"I am telling you, son of my father. If you are worth your salt as a man, you will put this woman in her right position. A real man is not led by a nose-ring leash," said Ndoda, hitting the restaurant table so hard that he drew the attention of other customers.

"I hear you my Big Brother, the Brave One. It is not true that I am a weakling. It is quite difficult to tell these liberated women what to do. If they don't want something, you can't force them to," replied Rampho.

"Rubbish! My women listen to me. I say jump, they say how high. That is why I have never had a problem with them to date," said Ndoda, sinking his stained teeth into the steak he was eating. He never used fork and knife in his life. He feels those who do are the colonised weaklings. He was of the opinion that using hands was the best and the healthiest way a man can use to eat. He argued that food was prepared with bare hands in the first place.

"You are lucky Big Brother, the Brave One. I wish I was married to an obedient woman like yours," said Rampho.

"Nonsense, it is not a question of luck. It is how you treat them the moment you are married. If you allow her to have her way early in your marriage, you will find it difficult to change that later. You let this woman into your deep pocket, now you can't take her out," taunted Ndoda.

"You know. I should have insisted on taking my daughter to initiation school. That way she could have acquired the name of my aunt automatically," said Rampho.

"Exactly, that is where you blundered, son of my father. That is where you should have flexed your manhood, Preserving One!" exclaimed Ndoda.

"Yeah, I overlooked it since it is women's duty to initiate girls. I didn't foresee this complication," said Rampho.

"I think the only way you can appease the ancestors is by taking a second wife," suggested Ndoda.

"Take a second wife, huh?" Rampho asked, sounding perplexed.

"Yes. Why not? Besides, this woman failed to bear you an heir. Maybe the second one will give you that blessing. This cheeky one will also become obedient once she realises that she has competition," said Ndoda.

Rampho was mum for a while. He took a deep breath and straightened up in his chair.

"Maybe that is not a bad idea at all, but the problem is, will the current wife agree?" said Rampho.

"Stop being timid, Preserving One!" exclaimed Ndoda, "you convince her. You are the one who suited and persuaded her to marry you. How can you fail to do likewise now or did she approach you first?" mocked Ndoda.

"No! How could you think that? I am the man of course. It is just that these modern women are not like our mothers. They marry us in community of property so we will find it difficult to walk out of the marriage. How could we be so stupid to fall into this obvious trap?" lamented Rampho.

"That is the problem with you the educated ones. You think when a woman calls you sweet names, cooks you the best meal you have ever tasted and massages you she truly loves you. She does all that to lead you into a life-time trap. Once she has you in the palm of her hand she shows her true colours. I will never be fooled by a woman," said Ndoda.

'You could say that again, Brave One. We are in a trap indeed. And the judges in the courts are biased towards them too. We are up against a vicious enemy and we are defenceless," bemoaned Rampho.

"I think we can change all that. If we as men become united and fight to reclaim our true position we could win the war. Yes, it seems farfetched but it is winnable" said Ndoda.

Rampho chuckled and sipped a mug of beer.

"If only we could have law makers on our side, but that is not possible because they do not experience the difficulties we are going through on the ground. Besides, they have populated the parliaments with women. It is not going to be possible to even suggest amendment of those anti-man laws," said Rampho.

"You are right there, Preserving One. Those male political leaders would do anything to get a smile from a woman," Rampho rejoined.

The two men finished their mugs of beer and walked out of the restaurant. They parted ways promising to call each other again to arrange for another meeting.

"You educated people think that your friends matter more than your own flesh and blood. What happened to the old adage that blood is thicker than water?" joked Ndoda.

"It is not only the educated ones. The uneducated are worse," Rampho said, laughing and getting into his car.

9

Mpho returned to university on Sunday and on her arrival she felt unusual. She had stomach cramps and felt nauseous. She didn't understand what was going on with her body. She rushed to the bathroom and vomited. One of the girls was in the bathroom and she jokingly suggested that she was pregnant. Mpho didn't pay attention to her comment as she knew that she used protection all the time. The nausea persisted for three days until she decided to visit a doctor. To her surprise the doctor diagnosed that indeed she was pregnant. She was utterly shocked. She fell silent and motionless for a while.

"How could this have happened?" she mused.

The first person that she wanted to talk to was her mother. She dialled her number and when she heard her voice on the other side she burst into tears. Her mother wanted to know what was wrong but could not get a clear answer. Mpho was shaking like a leaf. Her hands were sweating and everything went blank. When she woke up she was in one of the consultation rooms of the doctor's surgery.

"You fell unconscious, but it is fine you are in good hands," said the voice of a young medical practitioner, with a reassuring smile on his face, "it is normal for a young person to react the way you did after finding out that they were pregnant."

Mpho realised that it was not a bad dream. It was as clear as daylight that she was going to be a mother. She felt that she was not ready for the gruelling task of motherhood. She had vowed to finish her studies before she considered having children.

She didn't want to tell anyone yet. It would be her little secret until it had become impossible to keep it under wraps. She rejected Funkel's calls and avoided him on campus. When she did bump into him she would run away like a lunatic. Funkel didn't understand what was going on with the love of his life. He tried to find out from her friends but all that proved fruitless. They were as equally astounded by her emotional vicissitude. All they could tell him was that they hardly saw her as she had suddenly become withdrawn and moody. They tried to fish out the cause of the state of affairs without success.

Mpho, the jolly and noisiest girl on campus had all of a sudden become taciturn. "Mpho, what is eating you up girl? We are your friends you can trust us with anything," said Dineo trying to reassure her friend.

"Yes, Dineo is right. Friends cover each other's backs. We have never let you down in the past. How can we stoop that low now?" asked Koketso. Mpho sobbed and tears welled up in her eyes and rolled down her face like a waterfall. Dineo covered her in her arms and she was crying too. "Shhh...shh. Please don't cry girlfriend. I can't bear to see you like this. Please let us know what is wrong. We can only be able to help if we know what is eating you inside," she said, in the midst of sniffs.

The two friends truly loved their friend and were concerned about her well-being. They also became depressed as Mpho's stress had infected them like a flu virus. They realised that it would affect their studies as they hardly concentrated in class. Mpho had missed several lessons which became a major concern.

"Is it about your attack or has your boyfriend done something wrong to you? He will have to answer to us. We will definitely make life a living hell for him. He will wish he was never born," threatened Koketso.

"The spoilt brats, they think we are cheap. How could he play with your feelings like that?" said Dineo.

"No. He didn't do anything. It is me. I have been stupid," said Mpho reverting to jerky sniffs.

"If a girl cries like that, there could be only one reason. Boys problems!" said Koketso emphatically.

"It is fine girlfriends. I will be fine really. Thanks for your concern.

You have shown me that you are true friends indeed," said Mpho wiping tears with the palm of her hand.

"We will never let go of you until you tell us what is wrong? You are a mess Mpho. It kills us to see you like this," said Dineo.

"I shall tell you when the time is right. Right now all I need is a space to clear my mind, please!" begged Mpho. She had stopped crying but her eyes were bloodshot and swollen.

"Okay, we shall leave you for now but tomorrow you tell us or else we call your mother," said Koketso.

"Thanks for your understanding. All I need now is a soothing shower and a seven hours sleep. I will see you tomorrow guys," Mpho said.

Mpho sauntered to her room ruminating about the number of people she had let down if they were to know about her condition. These included among others her parents, friends, relatives, church elders and bursary funders. All these people had faith in her and never doubted her integrity. All that would evaporate like morning dew at sunrise when the truth came to light.

She had to act fast and contrive a solution to the problem.

She overheard certain girls talking about legal abortion one time. She logged on the internet on her laptop for more information on the subject. She down-loaded the contact details of clinics and gynaecologists who offered that service professionally. She heard a lot about botched abortions that irreparably damaged or even killed many women and girls. She dreaded the worst-case scenario.

She weighed another option of giving birth secretly and abandoning or giving up the child for adoption. How she would conceal her pregnancy from ogling eyes of young people on campus was a rocky mountain to climb.

As she was lost in her world of thoughts her cellular phone rang and she jolted as she was caught off guard. It was Funkel calling. She merely looked at it until it stopped ringing. It rang several times and she only ignored it. She vowed not to talk to him anymore. Poor Funkel was going through hell trying to figure out what the problem was. He even turned to an unlikely ally, Jaas. He was so keen to find out the truth that he seemed despondent.

"You must thank your lucky stars that she showed you her true colours this early. You didn't want to believe us when we told you that these people are bad news. Now we have been vindicated that we are good judges of character. First she put you in hospital, now she has dumped you like garbage," said Jaas.

Funkel was confused. He realised that he came to a wrong messiah.

"I have a bad feeling about this. There must be more than meets the eye here. I shall not rest until I get to the bottom of it. I will leave no stone unturned I promise you. If she doesn't want to be with me anymore, why doesn't she say so? I mean, she could simply SMS the painful message to say the least," said Funkel.

"Come on buddy! Let her go. Can't you read between the lines?" said Jaas taunting him.

"You don't understand. I really love this girl. My life is as good as finished without her," insisted Funkel.

"You can't force her to be a decent person. You aren't even compatible. Let her go man!" said Jaas emphatically.

"I wouldn't do that even if she told me to my face that she didn't want us to be together anymore. I would rather be dead," said Funkel.

"You are bewitched, man. All you need is exorcism," said Jaas, with a chuckle.

The two boys could not come to a conclusive reasoning until they parted. Jaas promised Funkel that he would find out the truth for him before the end of that week. He was intent on keeping his tabs on Mpho for the sake of his old friend. He thought maybe the truth would make him return to the fold.

The task Jaas was commissioned to perform came in handy in the object of bringing the Funkel train back on the rails.

He seized the golden opportunity to display his expertise.

Mpho had, in the meantime, made up her mind to have a legal abortion. She made a booking at a clinic through e-mail. She was advised to go through counselling in preparation for the procedure. Everything seemed to be on track until Jaas sneaked into her room while she was attending classes. He had somehow got hold of her attendance time-table. Breaking into Mpho's room was like a walk in the park as Jaas was an expert in lock picking.

As a Computer Science student he effortlessly hacked into Mpho's laptop. As he was browsing through the history folder of her internet explorer he stumbled upon a cracking revelation. She had logged onto abortion clinics websites, sent and received e-mails. He swiftly copied all the information to his data storage flash-drive. Funkel would be blown away by his finding, he thought.

A certain girl came into Mpho's room and found Jaas busy on her computer. He had forgotten to lock the door when he entered. He quickly told the girl that he was sent there by Mpho to look at her computer. The girl seemed to believe him and she went away without suspecting anything disconcerting.

Jaas personally logged onto the website of the e-mailed clinics to peruse full details. He requested one of his girl-friends to call the clinics for a bogus appointment.

Funkel, meanwhile, bumped into Mpho in the corridor of the Administration Centre. She tried to avoid him but Funkel pursued her like her own shadow until she relented.

"Please! Funkel, forget about me. Just go on with your life. It is for the best," she said, looking away.

"I demand to know the reason for this sudden change. Is it anything that I have done or what my parents said at the hospital? Please tell me because it is killing me. You know I love you with all my being," said Funkel, trying to hold her hand in his. She quickly withdrew her hand, clutching her books with both hands to avoid contact. She looked nervous as she was trembling. Her eyes were dilated and watery. She was about to burst into tears. A stream of tears rolled down her cheeks.

"We are two different people," she said, sniffing and wiping tears off her face. Funkel offered her a handkerchief, "our relationship will never work. Our people and parents in particular, will never give us their blessings. I have seen your parents the other day, they hate my guts. How will they accept me if our relationship should go further?" she enquired hesitatingly.

"Thank you babe, I didn't know that you were also thinking of marriage in the future as well. There is no better proof that we love each other and are compatible," said Funkel with a teasing smile. He was able to extract a smile from Mpho.

"You naughty boy!" she said shyly.

"I am glad you are now smiling again. You know your smile is like rain after a severe drought. It waters my dry and lonely heart. Your happiness is the essence of my being," said Funkel stroking her shoulder. She giggled. Her smile was paradoxical because her eyes told a story of torture.

"Let no other people's attitudes determine what we need. Our love should be insulated against racial slurs and jealousy. We are the only pilots of this plane or captains of our ship of love," said Funkel. She nodded her head now and then.

"It is just that sometimes I feel that you might not be ready for this," said Mpho.

"Ready for, what? Are you crazy? I know what I want. I am over eighteen, remember? I know what I am doing," said Funkel.

"It is just that there are certain things that might happen and I am scared you will leave me. I don't want to be a laughing-stock," said Mpho, touching her tummy unconsciously.

"Nonsense, I will never leave you no matter what happens or who says what. To me you are like water to a fish. I can't survive without you," said Funkel.

"Do you really mean what you are saying?" she asked suspiciously.

"I mean every word I say. I can't wait for the day we complete our studies and start working. We will then plan our first baby. I wish it would be a girl. I love baby girls. I have never had a sister so she will compensate for all that," said Funkel with a smile on his face. He was staring in the distance imagining the future that was seemingly still far away.

Mpho's mood quickly changed and she started walking away. Funkel noticed it and thought he said something that irritated her. "What is wrong now? I am sorry. Silly me," he said apologetically.

"It is nothing. I will see you tomorrow. I have to go to the library to prepare for the test I am writing in two days' time," she said running away.

Funkel was astounded but relieved to hear that she would see him again. He turned and walked to his dormitory whistling a medley of unknown songs. He had a slight spring in his gait. He occasionally ran and kicked the air. He seemed rejuvenated.

Mpho quickened to her room, she locked the door and threw herself on the bed. She cried herself to sleep. She was awakened by her neighbour Mercy knocking on her door.

She staggered to the door and opened it. "Hey, girl I have been knocking on your door for ages. I knew you were inside because the key was in the keyhole. What's up?" asked Mercy.

'Ah! I am fine. I have been to the library, so I am just tired. That is all," Mpho said slumping on the bed.

"You are right. We can't afford to relax and fail. Hard work breeds success. Besides there are many people who count on us and also those who will be happy to see us fail," Mercy said encouragingly.

Mpho nodded her head in agreement. She unconsciously touched her belly and seemed absorbed in meditation. Mercy could see that something wrong was afoot. She had known her for a while to notice if there was something wrong with her.

"By the way, I found a certain white guy in here about thirty minutes ago fiddling with your laptop. Did you ask anyone to come and fix it for you?" asked Mercy.

"You found a white guy in my room? No. I didn't send anyone to repair my laptop. There is nothing wrong with it. I am surprised. What did he look like?" asked Mpho.

"He is not the one who used to come here with you, but they are of the same age and height," said Mercy.

"Have you seen him before?" asked Mpho seeming more worried.

"Yes, his face seemed familiar. I must have seen him somewhere. I just don't remember where but if I see him again I will recognise him. This is worrying, girl. Is anything missing?" asked Mercy seeming more concerned.

"No. Everything seems to be at its right place. Let me check the laptop maybe there is something there," said Mpho, opening her laptop and switching it on. She found nothing wrong with it. All her files were intact.

It remained a disturbing mystery. She called home and spoke with both her parents. They sounded fine and she didn't want to bother them with what had happened. She only told Funkel who also seemed taken aback.

Funkel suspected Jaas and he went straight to his room to enquire. Jaas didn't deny anything. "You will be blown away by what I have discovered, buddy. It's way beyond expectations but it'll put you out of your misery," said Jaas jokingly.

"What are you talking about?" asked Funkel.

"You asked me to help you, didn't you? If you let me loose like a cannon fire, you must know that there will be an explosion. Once I am given a task I leave no stone unturned. We need to dig deeper if we are to get to the bottom," said Jaas, showing content with his own expertise.

"I didn't ask you to invade the privacy of my girlfriend. What you did is illegal. You could be arrested for doing that," said Funkel, "you have jeopardised my chances of getting her back because now she suspects that I am behind it," he said.

"Believe me, you would be better off without her," said Jaas.

"That is what you always wanted to achieve. It is self-fulfilling prophecy for you, isn't it?" complained Funkel.

As they were talking Jerome entered the room and announced that they expected the results of the elections the following day. "Guys, I suspect that REDYM rigged the elections. If they should win we are going to protest against the results. We cannot be fooled by minnows," said Jerome.

"No ways! I will not be led by communists. That will be the day. This is our fathers' university we cannot hand it over to corrupt scoundrels like that," said Jaas.

"Guys please! You have to let the democratic process take its course. If you are civil as you claim to be you will accept the results as free and fair. Let the best and most popular organisation win, guys," said Funkel, with a smile on his face.

"You are a traitor. You don't know which side your bread is buttered on," retorted Jaas.

"Yeah, the civilised world does not want back-stabbers like Funkel," added Jerome.

"Say what you want. All I know is that this world we live in has left the slow paced people like you far behind. You need to catch up or else you are going to be left in the swamp," said Funkel.

"Have you heard what they intent to do once they are re-elected? I heard from a reliable source that they intend to pressurise the management to restructure outsourcing of key services to this institution like catering, cleaning, security and supply of stationery. Can you believe that? And our dear friend here, does not know anything about it," said Jerome.

Funkel shook his head in disbelieve. "I don't know where you get this nonsense you are talking about. If that is done it will be a transparent process where all stake holders will have a contribution. I don't think it will be done without advertising in the mass media," said Funkel.

"Yeah, that is rich! Advertising will only be done for formality. They already know who they will give the tenders to, their cronies of course. The very corrupt officials who have mismanaged our public administration and also their mother party leeches," said Jaas.

"Tell me guys, do the current service providers represent the demographics of this country?" asked Funkel.

"They represent the best the country can offer. What do blacks know about the services concerned? They were taught how to perform those services by white people in the first place. How can they be better than those who taught them? They only know their indigenous services which are not suitable in this age of civilisation," said Jerome.

"Have you ever considered that there are people who are interested in those indigenous services you denigrate? Besides, having taught someone something does not mean that you are better. Your students can be innovative and creative to improve on what they learnt from you. That is the reason there are scholarships and new discoveries by young scholars. You are too dumb for a guy who claims to have the genes of intelligent ancestors," said Funkel.

"They can't beat us at our own game. When they learn the basics we will have perfected the skills. We will always be ahead of them no matter what," said Jaas.

"You are only paranoid guys. Remember whites were introduced to spices by Indians. Asian cooking is still the best. Do they monopolise what we learnt from them? We always give or take something from others. We are the only ones who patent our recipes. Other nations have allowed us access to their open secrets. It is a global village," said Funkel.

"We made that global village you are talking about. It is befitting that we should be the masters of that creation of ours. Why should we take the back seat now?" asked Jaas, showing signs of exasperation. Funkel could see fire in his eyes and tried to calm him down.

"We sometimes have to sacrifice or compromise for the sake of peace. If other nations were protective and selfish like we are, we wouldn't be having international trade for instance. We always expect others to go an extra mile while we hardly lift a finger to do likewise," said Funkel.

Funkel realised that the situation was becoming tense. He stood up as if he was going to the toilet and went to his own room.

The following morning was engulfed by bizarre red-faced sun sandwiched between the eye-lids of a dark cloud and a dark blue mountain range. There was something odd about the atmosphere. Mpho stretched and yawned wondering what the day had in store for the world. As she was wondering her cell phone rang heralding a new message. It was from the clinic confirming her appointment. Her heart throbbed irregularly as she pondered what it entailed. Funkel seemed not ready to be a father. He had never resisted using protection. She was blaming herself for all that happened. She would not jeopardise Funkel's chances of completing his studies by weighing him down with the burden of parenthood. The only person to bear the brunt of the sin was herself, she thought. She deliberately acted against her family values and norms. She relented to the devil's seduction. Her head was spinning with self-scolding that she resumed weeping. She cried her eyes dry.

She switched on her laptop to check her mail. There was a red flag on her computer which posited that there was new unread mail. It was a message from the psychologist she had made an appointment to see before the procedure. It was a point of no return, she thought. She had to bear that fleeting agony to save herself lifelong hardships. It was to be done stealthily and soon before other people close to her found out.

The waiting room at the psychologist's office was neatly polished. It was filled with sweet aroma of fresh flowers. The sofas were made of black velvet fabric and were comfortable with a reclining head rest. There was deafening silence that gave a tense mood. There was a young couple that looked like arch enemies. Tension between them could be touched with a hand. They looked so young it was surprising what could have spoiled their fledgling relationship. "Didn't they hear of couples that celebrated their fortieth anniversaries? Perfect relationships are as scarce as water in the desert nowadays. It seemed people were getting married so they could hurt each other or go through a divorce to gain popularity among their circle of friends," she mused. There was a new trend of divorce after-parties in the cities. Women divorcees were the ones wont to celebration of their regained freedom. The cardinal reason for the parties was advertisement of their availability status to possible suitors.

When it was her turn to go in she hesitated. She was thinking of running out of the waiting room there and then. She stood up and dragged herself into the consultation room. The psychologist was a full woman in her early fifties. She was standing and smiling reassuringly, "Please have a sit," she said, "I am glad you came to see me," she said opening a file that was on her desk.

"I am confused," Mpho said. Dr Thozeni looked at her with soul piercing eyes as if reading her mind like a newspaper. Mpho looked down wiggling her hands. Dr Thozeni nodded her head in agreement.

"That is why you came to see me in the first place. Be free to say anything that troubles you. Your secret is safe with me. What is the matter," asked Dr Thozeni, pouring a glass of mineral water for her. She took a sip and put the glass down on the table. She had tears in her eyes. Dr Thozeni gave her chance to cry for a while. She stopped and wiped her tears with a handkerchief. She looked devastated. Dr Thozeni felt sorry for her.

"It is going to be fine," she said, "just tell me what the problem is. I will only help if you give me the details," she said.

"I...I am pregnant!" she burst out crying. Dr Thozeni stood up and stroked her shoulders.

"My baby, it is fine. People make mistakes. I know how horrifying it is to be in your condition. Tell me, is your boyfriend supportive of you?" she asked.

"No. He doesn't even know I am pregnant," Mpho replied.

"You should tell him. He has the right to know that you are carrying his child," said Dr Thozeni.

"I tried but he seemed not ready to carry the responsibility. I could deduce that from his utterances.

That is the reason for my decision to abort the baby,"
she said, sobbing.

"It is wrong to jump to conclusion without getting
your facts straight first. You might be surprised to find
that the contrary happens. I am going to ask you to
first tell him and hear his reaction. You don't have to
hide your decision from him as well. This must be a
mutual decision. It could have far reaching
consequences for both of you," she said now swinging
in her chair.

They continued their conversation chatting about
general light stuff. When Mpho came out of the
session she felt light and could afford a smile. She
went to a popular fast food restaurant to grab
something to ease her hunger.

While she was waiting to be served, she gathered
courage to send Funkel an SMS inviting him to join her
at the restaurant as she had something very important
to talk about. He arrived in about ten minutes' time.
He found her reading a comic book.

"Hi! What is the matter? I came as soon as I could," he
said pulling a chair and sitting. A waiter saw him sit
and attended to him quickly. He gave him a menu
book to place his order.

"This is going to be on you I suppose," he said jokingly.
Mpho shrugged her shoulders and displayed a quick
crescent smile.

"I am kidding. I have been longing to give you a treat
myself, but you wouldn't let me," he said with a
chuckle.

"Get out of here! You are the meanest man I have ever known," she said, chuckling.

"Ah, how many men do you know?" asked Funkel with a frown.

"You are going to collapse if I should let you know," she said dismissingly.

"That cannot be true. You are the most inexperienced girl I have ever dated," said Funkel teasingly.

"How many girls have you dated before you met me?" asked Mpho, poising as if ready to strangle him.

"Let me think," touching his chin, "nah, I don't want to lose you," he said, laughing.

"You, silly!" exclaimed Mpho.

Mpho sat down and they chatted for hours on end. She wanted to break the news to him but failed to gather courage. Every time she thought of it words would stick in her throat. Funkel ultimately asked her what she wanted to talk to him about that seemed so urgent. She only said that she wanted to spend some time with him. "We haven't seen each other in a while. Is it a sin to want to see my most favourite man in the whole world?" she asked, giving him her ravishing look.

"Of course not, it is just that you sounded a little anxious," he said, taking her hand in both his.

"If I sounded otherwise you would not have come, would you?" she asked accusingly.

"What? Are you kidding me? I would swim across the Atlantic to come to see you at any time you called. I live for you. You are going to be the mother to my children when we complete our studies. I intend to keep you happy forever," he said, stroking and kissing her hand.

The waiter came and asked if they wanted to order again. They realised that they had overstayed in that restaurant. They stood up and Funkel paid the bill and Mpho gave the waiter a tip. Funkel joked that he didn't know she was that loaded and generous. If he knew he would not have bothered paying for the food they ate, he said.

On the way Mpho was quiet and gave the excuse that she was tired.

10

The results of SRC elections were released and the REDYM got a resounding victory. There were outcries against elections results. The losing student organisations and candidates accused the winners of election rigging. A formal complaint was lodged with the elections officer for a re-counting of the ballot papers or a re-run of the elections.

A protest march to the Administration Block was organised by concerned groups. It was supposed to be a peaceful march but things got out of hand when members of REDYM tried to intervene. Violent clashes ensued and several students sustained serious injuries. The campus security personnel could not quell the clashes so the management had to call in the police. Several students were arrested. Jaas was among those incarcerated. They were charged with incitement, damage to property, assault with intention to do grievous bodily harm and possession of dangerous weapons.

Calm returned to the campus but the situation remained tense for a while. The police maintained their visibility on campus to circumvent another retaliatory eruption of clashes. The detained students were locked in the holding cells of the local police station and appeared before a magistrate the following day. They were remanded in custody as the prosecution felt their release could make the clashes flare up.

©PJ Ntsoane

There was a turn of events as Jaas and others were required to join in an identity parade. It emerged that they were linked to other criminal offences committed in the area.

Jaas was positively linked to an assault crime. This conclusion was made after positive identification by an eye witness and forensic report made on a golden wrist watch that fell at the scene as they were making their get-away after attacking Funkel and his girlfriend. Jaas was not even aware that his watch was missing because he had several of them. He was bundled into a police car and driven to the campus where his room was searched in his presence. A balaclava and a wide assortment of assault weapons were found in his room. He was made to disclose names of his accomplices. They were also rounded up and taken to prison.

Funkel was surprised when he was contacted and told that his attackers were found. He picked up Mpho and rushed to the police station where he was given a date and time of their appearance. They were refused permission to see the suspects. They were so excited that their attackers would finally be brought to book.

On the day of the first appearance Funkel and Mpho were very surprised to find Jaas, Jerome and Trotsky among a group of the five accused of the crime.

"This is an odd combination," Funkel said to Mpho, "I didn't expect arch enemies like those to suddenly become comrades in arms."

"We are an odd combination as well, remember? The enemy of your enemy is your friend," she said.

"Oh, now I see. You clever head!" he said poking her on the head.

"I am an attorney in training, don't forget," she said smiling.

"We have to make this work, babes. Our love was meant to change hardened attitudes. If we could make those ones work together, what about the majority who could be positively influenced? We can contribute to national reconciliation," he said.

"Maybe we should drop the charges. They hardly expect it, so it might make them see reason," she suggested, looking Funkel in the eyes.

"You are right sweet heart," he said, "but let's make them feel the pinch a little bit," he suggested.

They allowed the legal process to continue for two sessions and then applied for charges to be dropped. The accused could not believe their ears when they heard that their case had been withdrawn on humanitarian grounds. The defendants' lawyer had studied the merits of the case and knew that the law was not on their side. They thanked both Funkel and Mpho endlessly.

Funkel's father was only convinced that the white boys were innocent. He insisted that Trotsky and the other two black boys were the only culprits in the case. He was fuming when he heard that the charges were withdrawn.

"How could my boy let those criminals walk free?" Piet asked Debora, "they should rot in jail for heaven's sake," he sneered.

"He is confused Dad. He is only doing it to please that girlfriend of his. I pray that he should use protection if he ever gets tempted. Those people have loose morals. She will ultimately seduce my boy," said Debora, clutching the Holy Book in her hands.

"We must take him out of that university. This affair is going to interfere with his studies. I think we should send him to a European University," he said.

"You are right Dad. We must take him far away where the *muti* of that little witch will not reach him," she added angrily.

"We must ask the priest and the congregation to pray for him. Maybe their prayers will be heeded by God," he said.

The two sat together silently staring in the distance. A dog was chasing a cat in the backyard. The dog pursued the cat persistently and never stopped even though it looked more powerful. The cat climbed a tree and the dog sat under it, barking incessantly. The cat was so scared that it leaped onto the ground and dashed for cover, with the dog in hot pursuit. The cat realised that it was cornered so it turned and faced the assailant. It gave several fierce jabs. The dog retreated wailing with its tail between the legs.

Piet was watching all that when it happened and gave a howling laughter. He described all that he saw to his wife who was not paying attention to the action. She nodded and chuckled intermittently in amazement. "God works in mysterious ways. The weak and persecuted are always given strength to fight back," he said.

"That is why David defeated Goliath," Debora replied.

"God was on his side despite his physical disadvantage. It shows that God's power surpasses all," Piet said.

It was time for the news on the radio and Piet never missed a news bulletin. He was wont to mumble and utter abuse whenever he heard something he disapproved of. What acutely riled him was any mention of a criminal activity, especially when the suspect was black. He would say, 'Typical of them!' It was mentioned that Laager University had been temporarily closed due to violent activities and boycott of classes. "This is only happening because blacks have been allowed to study at Laager. It is unlikely for all white institutions to be entangled in petty squabbles that lead to violent activities. Lazy black students are the cardinal source of problems. They are wasting our children's time," said Piet angrily.

"You could say that again. We have only experienced deterioration of standards since the so-called racial integration process was introduced. It will never work!" Debora said emphatically.

"Decency is foreign to blacks. All they want is free this and free that. They don't want to work," said Piet.

"When white graduates leave this country for greener pastures and security overseas, they complain of brain drain or accuse them of being unpatriotic," said Debora.

"There is no self-respecting intellectual who is worth his salt who can work in a country like this. There is this ridiculous Black Affirmation Policy which denies whites employment opportunities. It is pure racism. If this madness is not stopped, the best will always go away," Piet said, lighting his tobacco pipe. Debora did not like her husband's habit.

She was asthmatic and would always move away from him whenever he lit his pipe.

"Daddy, you must consider quitting smoking. It is not good for your health. Look at your teeth, they look like an old chimney," complained Debora.

"Stop it woman! My great-grand parents smoked and nothing wrong happened to them. I took after them. This is like a culture to us. It is a symbol of manhood. Your sissy of a son seems to be breaking the norm. No wonder he behaves like he does," said Piet, taking a lungs-full puff and emitting a huge smoke that covered his head like a cloud on top of Mount Kilimanjaro.

"He is not doing all that he does because he is a non-smoker," she said.

"What is it then? Smoking makes a man!" roared Piet.

"I think it is the bad influence he got. He was always in the company of children from liberal families. They are the ones who did the damage," argued Debora.

"I failed him as a father. I should have exerted the right influence myself," said Piet, looking sad.

"It is never too late to mend. All is not lost. We must not stop trying. He will see reason at the end," said Debora, trying to console her husband.

As they were busy talking a car pulled up at the gate and hooted. Funkel got out and the remote controlled gate slid open.

"It must be because of the disturbances at Laager," said Piet.

"At least my child is safe," said Debora, "I was so worried about him."

"If anyone dared touch my boy, I would kill them with my bare hands," said Piet, clenching his fists.

"I don't like his political leanings though," said Debora. Funkel came to the veranda where his parents were sitting.

He greeted and hugged them. "It has been a long drive I am exhausted. I need a rest," he said dashing back into the house.

"We must invite the Vermeulens over to dine with us tomorrow. I like their daughter Marita so much. She could be a perfect match for our Funkel. She is a well groomed *meisie* who is full of respect and morals," said Debora.

"Nothing will make me happier than a Volk daughter-in-law. I spend sleepless nights worrying about this boy's preferences. God, please hear my prayers!" said Piet, with eyes closed and both hands clasped together.

"God will answer our prayers in the best way at the right time. I know my God will never fail us," said Debora.

The Vermeulens honoured the invitation. Marita also attended. Debora tried desperately to set them off talking to each other. Funkel sensed what his parents were up to and played along. The two chatted and laughed together. They seemed to have a good time.

The Vermeulens thanked their hosts and promised to return their superb hospitality.

Funkel showed his courtesy by walking Marita to the car. His parents were positive about the possibility of a relationship developing between the two youngsters. They only needed a little push in the right direction, it seemed.

When they were gone, Debora commented about Marita's good assets. "A young man who will marry her will be the luckiest on earth," she said, staring at Funkel as if to read his facial expression.

"I agree with you Mom. She is a great girl with perfect sense of humour. She is definitely going to make someone a very happy husband," said Funkel, nodding his head in agreement.

"Don't you want to be that lucky man, my son?" asked Piet.

"No. She is not my type," said Funkel curtly.

"You are going to marry a wrong girl if you let this one slip away. You need to hurry up before it is too late," said Debora.

"You will see how good I am at choosing a life partner. You will not be disappointed," said Funkel, giggling mischievously. His parents looked at each other and simultaneously shook their heads. They realised they had to work hard to achieve their dream of getting their heir his perfect match.

The following day was the day Mpho was booked to go through with abortion at the clinic. She was so nervous that she called Funkel in an attempt to calm her nerves. She told him how she loved him and would do anything to make him happy. Funkel returned the sweet words accordingly and did not suspect anything.

On the day of the appointment she went to the clinic alone. She sat on the chair in the waiting room. She was trembling and it seemed everybody knew what she was there to do. She felt as if they were judging her and condemning her to hell.
"It is not their body this. The decision on what to do is solely mine," she thought.
She sent Funkel messages on the cell phone and told him how she loved him. Funkel asked her if there was anything wrong and she always had no courage to say what was eating her up.
The nurse called her name twice before she could respond. It was time for her to go into surgery. She kept on looking at the door hoping someone would walk in and stop her from going through with the

procedure. Everything seemed to move in slow motion. She was a little disorientated. She felt like she was in an alien environment on a different planet. Nobody seemed to care. She was on her own and vulnerable.

She was ordered to take off her clothes and jewellery before lying on the bed. She nervously looked around the room and saw big strange machines, lights, syringes, scissors and knives. Her heart was pounding like a bass drum and she shivered like a leaf. She put on the hospital gown and lay on the bed ready for the surgery to begin. She closed her eyes and said a short prayer. When she opened her eyes she heard a commotion outside the room. People were arguing and someone threatened to call in the police. The door to the room flung open. "Please, please, don't go through with it! I love you and I will take care of you and the baby," Funkel said, throwing himself over Mpho.

Funkel got down on one knee, "Mpho, you are the love of my life. I don't know what I would do if I lost you. Our relationship is the best thing that ever happened to me. Will you marry me? I don't have the ring with me now but it is here in my heart," said Funkel. The whole clinic staff had gathered in the room. The bulky security guards had frozen in action.

"Yes, yes, my love, I will marry you!" she exclaimed. Everybody who was watching burst in applause.

"When Jaas called me last night I quickly came over to stop you from doing the most terrible mistake of your life," Funkel said.

"Jaas?" she asked in amazement. She knew Jaas to be totally against mixed relationships. He was the last person she expected to rescue her relationship with Funkel.

"It is a long story. I will tell you at the right time. Now let us get out of this place and go to town and celebrate our sweet victory," Funkel suggested.

Jaas was waiting for them in the car parked outside the clinic.

"I do not approve of your relationship. It is just that I couldn't let an innocent life end so abruptly. Besides I have nothing to lose. It was my way of thanking you for withdrawing the charges against us. I am not a bad person after all," said Jaas, who was leaning against his father's German made car.

"There is a little bit of humanity in you after all. Thank you very much dude. I owe you for this one. You are a true friend indeed," said Funkel.

"It is my pleasure," Jaas said, bowing in appreciation, "you must take good care of them. One wrong step you will have to answer to me," he said, giggling and getting into his car and drove away at breath taking speed. The two love birds stood together, waving and watching the car squeaking away. They walked hand in hand towards Funkel's Italian made luxury car that he borrowed from his uncle Louis, who happened to be at his home when he got the most important message.

11

Mpho's parents were wondering where their child was because she didn't tell them anything before she left and her cell phone was off. They became anxious as they had realised that she was moody. They thought her condition was caused by traumatic events that happened to her and the closure of the university. She was known to be a peace loving girl.

"Honey, don't you have her friends' cell phone numbers?" asked Rampho.

"I had her friend Dineo's number in the SIM card of the phone that was stolen last week," said Mampho.

"Damn criminals! Nobody feels safe nowadays. Not even the policemen themselves. I have heard of a policeman who was mugged in broad day light in town last week. If this happens to the police who are armed law enforcers, what about us?" Rampho asked rhetorically.

"I think death sentence should be reinstated. It will be the only deterrent. These scumbags have turned our streets and homes into their own domain," added Mampho.

"I think death sentence will be too excessive if applied to petty crimes. I know that only blacks will fall victim to the hangman's noose. Whites will always be given light sentences or acquittal for their criminal activities. The courts of law in this country are still dominated by biased judges," said Rampho.

"That is not true. Judges apply the rule of law objectively. They give their verdict according to the merits of the case or evidence brought forward," she said.

"You know nothing about those people. They will always find excuses like, psychiatric imbalances or mistaken identity in mitigation for their fellows. It is a norm for them," he said.

As they were busy arguing Mpho came into the house. She looked exhausted but her face was radiant. "We were worried about you. Where have you been?" asked Mampho.

"I have been to town. I had something important to take care of," Mpho replied.

"But still you should have told us. You cannot just up and go. People are kidnapped nowadays. Haven't you heard about human trafficking? There is word about this notorious Mr Bling who targets vulnerable young girls. It is not safe walking alone in town under the circumstances," said Rampho.

"I can take care of myself Dad, don't worry. Besides, I am a black belt karateka," she said.

"Who said that karateka experts cannot be overpowered? If you were saying that God protects you it would have been better. It shows that you have faith in your own strength. What is wrong? Are you becoming an atheist?" said Mampho.

"God helps those who try, Mom. You cannot just fold your arms when attacked and expect God to perform miracles for you. If you run away God will help you to outrun your attackers. If you fight back God will also make you repel your attackers. I believe in God Almighty and His only begotten son Jesus by the Virgin Mary. I couldn't be an atheist even if I tried," said Mpho.

"You must be careful not to be an impulsive shopper like your mother. She blows the whole credit card limit in a day," said Rampho.

"Look who is talking. He is the one who is black listed because he is the poorest personal finance manager I have ever known," replied Mampho, laughing her lungs out.

"You have short memory. You must remember that you were the one who did not give me time to breathe about things that had to be bought in this house. You would complain about this and that which you had seen at some of your friends' houses. You would make me feel guilty so you could have your way. In fact you blackmailed me into bankruptcy," retorted Rampho.

"That is all lies. You never bought anything in this house. I personally have no clue what you are doing with your money. I sometimes become suspicious that you must be having a mistress somewhere," said Mampho.

"If I had one you wouldn't be so fresh," said Rampho.

"Cut it you two!" Mpho shouted, "I wonder why this is escalating into mud-slinging," she said. As soon as she finished saying those words her cell phone rang. It was Funkel telling her to inform her parents about the visit his parents intend to make to meet hers. "Mom, Dad! I have something to tell. Please, calm down as this may shock you," said Mpho.

"What is the matter child? You look troubled," said Rampho.

"No, I am not troubled. It is just that what I have to say is serious. The phone call I have just received..." said Mpho.

"The phone call, what about it? Who was it?" interrupted Mampho.

"Please! Let me finish," pleaded Mpho.

"Alright child, what is it?" intervened Rampho.

"It was Funkel. He says that his parents are coming to pay us a visit," Mpho said, fixing her eyes on the floor.

"Is this Funkel the one with whom you were attacked?" asked Rampho.

"Yes, he is the one," said Mpho.

Mpho's parents had no clue what the visit was about. They only assumed that it concerned the attack. Mpho did not even disclose to her mother the purpose of the visit. She could only sense, as a mother would, that there was something more to it. She didn't want to overwhelm her daughter with questions either.

Preparations for their guests got underway forthwith. They had never had white guests in their house before.

"We must prepare our best. I don't want them to look down upon us. We must show them that we are a civilised family. I will cook the best Greek or sea food there is. I must buy a cook book. Mpho you must come with me to town too..." Mampho was so ecstatic and confused at the same time.

"Please, Mom. There is no need to panic. Just be yourselves. They will only look down upon you if you try hard to be who you are not. They will only respect you for being true Africans," Mpho quipped.

"Mpho is right. She is so clever. She has taken after me. What difference will it make if you give them what they already know? They need to experience new things," added Rampho.

"Get out of here. You have never said or done anything clever in your entire life. There can be only one person here that she took after," taunted Mampho.

"Say what you like. The fact is we know who is the brains behind the success of this household," retorted Rampho.

"Stop your petty squabbles. You know my chromosomes are from both of you. You act like uneducated people," said Mpho.

"But my genes are obviously the dominant ones," replied Rampho.

"If yours were dominant, she wouldn't have passed the twelfth grade. You struggled to pass yours yourself," said Mampho.

Rampho stood up and left the room because he realised he would not win the argument. He never did. He went outside on the balcony to watch the sunset. He enjoyed the golden sight of the horizon as the sun patiently disappeared down the mountain-side far away. He loved the sight of birds flocking to their nests to rest and feed their nestlings. He imagined how happy the young ones would be when the parents arrived home safely. He also thought sadly about those which would fail to arrive home either as a result of having fallen victim to beasts of prey or being caught in various man made traps. The night would be lonely and traumatic for those affected. He prayed silently, "God, please shield the innocent against harm."

The Koekemoers arrived early on a partly cloudy Saturday morning. They were smartly dressed. Piet dressed in a black tuxedo, a pure white silk shirt with a matching black tie and a black trilby hat.

Debora was wearing a blue frilled long sleeve dress and a sun-hat. She was wearing a pearl chain and black high heel shoes.

Rampho was wearing his stone red West African suit and sandals. Mampho was in blue Pedi traditional dress and also wearing sandals with laces up her shin.

They welcomed their guests with broad smiles at the gate.

"Welcome to our humble abode," Rampho said with a smile.

They shook hands and walked into the house. Mampho offered them tea with cookies that she had baked the night before.

They drank the fresh *rooibos* tea and chatted for hours on end.

"Mr Rampho, our coming here was not only about the unfortunate incident that happened to our children," Piet said, pausing to take a deep breath, "our son, Funkel asked us to come and negotiate with you for your daughter's hand in marriage."

Rampho nearly fainted in his chair. His hand froze in mid-air holding a stuffed protein rich *mopani* worm in his hand.

"Excuse me! Did you say marriage?" asked Rampho, with surprise written all over his face.

"Yes, our son would like to marry your daughter. That is the reason why we are here," said Piet.

"It is impossible! She told me that they were only friends. She lied to me. I don't know what to say about this. If I would give you my opinion, I personally do not approve of this. She is still a baby. Besides, they still have to finish their studies," said Rampho.

"My point exactly, I don't think it would be appropriate for them to rush into such a serious commitment. Let us encourage them to take their time. They will soon come to their senses and realise that it was a passing whim," said Piet.

"You two go on as if we don't have a say in this matter. We, the women, also have a role to play here," said Mampho.

"In my culture women do not take part in marriage negotiations. You should know better," said Rampho.

"Of course, we have a say. They are our babies, we carried them for nine months and we suffered excruciating labour pains," added Debora. The two men looked at each other in surprise. They shook their heads in unison.

"It is not a question of who carried them for how long. That is how God created nature. God declared a man the head of the family. Are you two challenging His wisdom?" asked Piet.

"We didn't force Eve to sin against God in Eden," said Rampho.

"She had a good accomplice," retorted Mampho.

The two families argued about issues of procedure until time for the Koekemoers to leave arrived. They parted with mutual understanding of pursuing the matter but also dissuading the children from undertaking what they planned. They were not aware of the real reason for their children's decision to get married soon.

Funkel was anxiously waiting to hear what transpired. Upon arrival Piet and his wife called their son to the lounge.

"We are back, my son. We have seen your prospective in-laws as you insisted. But our impression is that they are totally different from us," said Piet.

"They eat with bare hands. And their food: Lord! They eat worms, tripe, chicken feet and intestines!" added Debora.

"I wonder if your girlfriend can use fork and knife at all. I don't know how you will cope because your girlfriend is seemingly incompatible," said Piet.

"Please, Dad, don't start. I am tired of arguing," said Funkel slumping in the sofa.

"How will she raise the *volk* children when she knows nothing about our culture?" said Piet, angrily.

"She is not going to raise your ideal *volk* children but ours. We come first, not an out-dated philosophy. We need to move with times, please," retorted Funkel.

"Happiness comes first. How are you going to spend the rest of your life with someone who does not make you happy?" asked Piet.

"Let me be the judge of that. It is my life you are talking about here, not yours," replied Funkel.

"Tell me, does she know anything about rugby or cricket? I am referring to the white-man's sports. A white man feels happy when talking, playing and watching these sports. Are you going to attend these with her? She will bore you to death. Please, my son, reconsider," begged Piet.

"For starters, I don't like those sports myself. Secondly I have never seen you and Mom go to those events together. Does she bore you? She never taught me those sporting activities herself. What do you say about that?" asked Funkel, with his arms folded and looking at his father with inquisitive eyes.

"Do not change the subject, son. We are discussing you, not me," said Piet.

"Dad, you cannot give me your old torn hat and worn out boots to wear. They will not be effective in present conditions like they were in the past. Let me get for myself the stuff that will suit my times. I will not change my mind, no matter what. Besides I wouldn't want my child to grow up without a father," said Funkel, unaware that he disclosed the secret. He put his hand on his mouth and patted his forehead with the palm of his hand when it dawned on him.

"What did you say?" asked Debora in astonishment.

"Okay, I have said it anyway. Mpho is pregnant with my child. That is why I want you to do whatever is necessary to enable us to be man and wife before the child is born," said Funkel.

"I don't believe this. How are you going to take care of the child when you are still at university? Do you expect us to carry your responsibility?" asked Piet, now on his feet pouring a glass of whisky.

"I will drop out if I have to. There is no way I am leaving my child out there. I will complete my degree through correspondence," threatened Funkel.

"Fine, you reap what you have sown. You brought this unto yourself," Piet concurred.

"No, Dad! We cannot jeopardise our son's future. There is something we can do," said Debora.

"Like what?" Piet asked, sipping his favourite drink.

"We could adopt the child until Funkel completes his studies.

©PJ Ntsoane

It will be better than marriage," suggested Debora.

"I am not adopting any half-caste child. What will my friends say? This boy thinks he is a man, let him be," said Piet

Funkel stood up and went to his bedroom upstairs. As he was climbing the stairs he said, "Fine I will deal with this my way. Don't say that I didn't try," said Funkel, disappearing upstairs.

Funkel decided to ask his uncle for help in the matter. He was one person who always came to his rescue whenever there seemed to be no help coming from his parents. His uncle was a modern and moderate man who despised racial discrimination and segregation. He had friends across racial lines and interacted with them at work. He worked in the entertainment industry and many of his colleagues were blacks.

He offered to have a word with Funkel's parents to convince them to support his favourite nephew. The talks bore no fruits as Piet was adamant. Uncle Louis decided to take matters up and start *magadi* negotiations with Mpho's elders.

Uncle Louis and Funkel went to Mpho's home. He insisted that the groom had to take part in the negotiations as well.

Uncle Louis convinced them, after softening them with a bottle of the most expensive whisky available, to compromise some of their traditional norms in the proceedings.

The bride's price was fixed at twenty cattle, thirty goats, ten sheep and five thousand rand. Funkel and his uncle tried in vain to have the livestock commuted to cash.

"The Malingas are members of the Lions clan royal family. Lions are carnivores. If you marry in our family you need to prove your bravery and manhood. You can only do that by bringing us what we demand for our daughter," said Ndoda, the brave one.

"Okay fine. We shall see what we can do," said Uncle Louis.

Funkel was quiet most of the time. He leaned towards his uncle, "These people are robbing us. How could they be so unfair to us? Where am I going to get all those animals from?" whispered Funkel, scratching his head in desperation and disbelief.

"You said you are a man. You either comply or kiss your girlfriend goodbye. It is up to you young man," said Uncle Louis. Funkel felt as if a huge boulder had been placed upon his shoulders. He was wondering where he was going to get all those animals without income or his father's help.

He was running against time. Soon Mpho would find it difficult to hide her pregnancy. Her mother had already commented about her waist line recently. She told her to watch her weight as she was developing a bulge around the waist.

"A girl makes a statement with her slim figure. Men, especially whites, like slender girls. Be careful or else your man is going to see other girls out there," said Mampho.

"My Funkel won't leave me irrespective of my weight. He adores me," Mpho said, prancing around the house as if she was modelling for a clothing line.

Mampho laughed and said, "Don't be too sure. You cannot trust boys of nowadays. They change their minds like the weather. The moment you think they are warm they suddenly fall to below zero," joked Mampho.

"Mine is not like that. I will strangle him," said Mpho.

"I am glad you trust him. I cannot bear to see you being heart-broken," said Mampho.

"Thank you, Mom. It is so sweet," said Mpho.

They both laughed and warmly hugged each other. It seemed like a cemented mother and daughter bond. Mpho knew deep in her heart that she was keeping something crucial from her mother. She was afraid to shatter her trust in her. She knew that if she dared reveal the secret her mother would run to her father and he would go ballistic. She couldn't risk spoiling the jolly atmosphere reigning in her house.

Her father was whistling happily in the backyard. He was watering his vegetable garden. It was his favourite domain.

Uncle Louis told Funkel's parents about their visit to the Malingas. Piet was so furious that Funkel disobeyed him and roped in his uncle to conclude marriage negotiations. He made it clear that he would not pay a cent or hand over his livestock to the greedy

Malingas who were intent on fleecing them just because they were white. He insisted that the marriage would not work as it was based on illusion.

"This boy is wasting our time and resources. He should be concentrating on his books instead of ogling at black girls' curves," said Piet, fuming.

"The children are truly in love. Denying them the right to live as man and wife will definitely drive them away or make them do something stupid," warned Uncle Louis.

Piet kept quiet for a while. He lit his pipe and blew a few puffs.

"Since there is going to be a child involved, separating them will be impossible. Let's do the prudent and give them what they want," pleaded Uncle Louis.

"Okay, I'll think about it, but I cannot promise you anything. Damn Funkel!" he exclaimed, hitting the table with his fist.

Meanwhile Funkel called Mpho on her cellular phone, "I don't believe how things are panning out now. Your parents have placed this huge tag on you. My father is unwilling to help and time is against us," said Funkel.

"How much did they ask for?" asked Mpho.

Funkel told her the price put on her. She laughed and Funkel felt embarrassed. "What is funny now?" asked Funkel, sounding confused.

"That is nothing. What did you expect, a free gift? They have gone too low if you ask me. If you love me you will make a plan," said Mpho.

"You don't seem to care. How could you support this unreasonable price?" inquired Funkel.

"You know I am worth far more than that. Do you care about the price or me?" asked Mpho.

"Of course I care about you. It is just that I feel they are trying to make it difficult for us to be together," said Funkel.

"You have to prove your manhood. Didn't you say that you would do anything to be with me? Now I am beginning to doubt you. Are you the man I fell in love with?" asked Mpho.

"What do you mean? Of course, I am. I am going to prove them wrong. I will marry you no matter what," said Funkel.

"I am relieved to hear that," said Mpho, giggling.

Funkel searched the internet for information on traditional marriages. He found a website on African traditional weddings. He read that a man was entitled to pay a certain percentage of the bride's price in case he could not acquire or afford the whole. He quickly called his Uncle Louis and asked for a loan. He requested him to arrange the initial proceedings of the marriage.

Uncle Louis was successful in convincing the Malingas to agree to a preliminary marriage before a priest in a church. They agreed that the traditional wedding would be done thereafter when Funkel was employed and able to earn income himself.

They thought that would defuse the necessity for their bright son-in-law to interrupt his studies.

A priest was found and a date set for the marriage made in heaven to finally take place. Mpho's parents were excited about the prospect of a marriage for their only child but Funkel's father made it clear that he would not give his blessings.

On the day of the wedding Mpho and her relatives packed the church to the rafters. Funkel was accompanied by his uncle and cousins. Piet refused to come and forbade his wife from accompanying her son on his big day. The poor woman nearly had a heart failure.

Funkel was very disappointed with his father and thanked God for Mpho's family. He failed to understand why his father would be so inconsiderate.

Mpho looked like an angel in her beautiful long dress. She had a beautifully braided hair with a ribbon held pony tail. Her make-up was done by a professional indeed, it was perfect. She smiled at Funkel who smiled back and whispered 'I love you' to her. Those in attendance were in a jolly mood. They were dancing, singing wedding songs and ululating vivaciously.

They went through the routines and exchanged vows. When the priest finally said 'You may kiss the bride' suddenly everybody fell silent. Their eyes were fixed towards the door. There stood Piet and Debora hand in hand. They arrived on time to hear the final declaration by the priest. They walked straight to the front and ascended the podium. The church was so quiet that everybody could hear one another's breaths and heart-beats.

Piet held the microphone in his hand. He looked around the church and fixed his eyes on the newly-weds. "I know many of you are surprised," he said, swallowing a lump in his throat, "I am the groom's father. I had taken a decision not to attend this wedding because of my personal views. It dawned on me that I am being selfish. My son is his own person. We parents often make a mistake of pressuring our children to be the ideal persons we dream about. We overlook the most important aspect, that they cannot live our lives. They have their own lives to live. I have made such a terrible mistake myself. I, therefore, ask for forgiveness from these two beautiful children of mine. I ask for forgiveness from the Priest, you the congregation and from God our Father. As a gesture of apology I have brought the entire bride's price asked by the Malingas. I know that your child Mpho is carrying my son's child," there was ululations and Mpho's parents looked at each other in surprise.

"I say to her, welcome to the family and I cannot wait to be a grandfather," he said to a cheerful applause and song. Funkel and Mpho were in tears hugging and kissing their parents.

"Why didn't you tell us that you were pregnant?" asked Mampho. Mpho looked at her and smiled, "I didn't want you to disown me," she joked. Her father was smiling from ear to ear. He was so excited that he was going to be a grandfather as well. His older brother Ndoda grabbed the microphone and asked for attention.

"As the head of the Malinga family, I would like to thank everybody for attending this ceremony. We didn't plan for a big wedding so we cannot promise you much. To the Koekemoer family I wish to say thank you for your interest in our daughter. We hope that this alliance will last forever. We know that we have raised a lady in our daughter, Mpho. She will not disappoint.

As regards your dowry, in our culture we do not send it back. We accept it with open arms and we will talk with your elders about the full wedding in the near future. And let me warn you though. In our culture we say a son-in-law never finishes marrying. You still owe us. Don't ever think you have paid up," he said, to a tumultuous laughter.

The celebrations went on at the Malingas' home until sunset. The Koekemoers mixed with the people from the township and neighbouring villages. It was a norm for close and distant relatives to converge to bear witness whenever one of them had a ceremony however big or small it was. The Malingas' relatives had come in droves. Men and women cooked traditional food in big pots to feed those in attendance.

They had slaughtered two goats, a sheep and five chickens for that small occasion. As descendants of the royal family of the neighbouring villages, their relatives were numerous.

Funkel and Mpho spent most of the day locked up in a room. They talked for hours on end and listened to singing and dance going on outside. Now and again a maiden relative would pop in to enquire about things they wanted to be supplied with. She made sure that they were never short of any supply.

"Did you know that in case I die young you will be expected to marry another girl from this family?" asked Mpho.

"What? We are going to grow old together. You are going nowhere," he said, giving her a kiss. She giggled and kissed him back. "In my tradition if the bride dies young or is unable to bear children, the family is supposed to give you another girl who will be your wife," she said.

"Don't tempt me," said Funkel, licking his lips.

"Don't get any wrong ideas, you dog," teased Mpho.

"I wouldn't mind, your girl relatives are very gorgeous, though they come nowhere near you," said Funkel.

Uncle Louis sent a message to Funkel telling him that they had to prepare to go on a honey moon. He had booked the most expensive suite for them at one of the five star hotels in the city. It was their surprise gift. They would spend two nights there. They were so excited. They stealthily got away to their destination.

They had a late night sleep. They were talking and hardly believed they were man and wife. It was not what they had planned to do so early in their lives.

"I don't believe I am a married woman. I wonder what my friends are going to say when they find out," said Mpho.

"First they are going to be shocked and then you will have to explain why you did not invite them to your wedding," said Funkel.

"The same applies to you. I haven't seen any of your friends at the church," replied Mpho.

"Well, they will have to understand. I had no choice. It all happened so fast. How will I have had a chance to invite them? Remember I was not sure it will become a reality. I mean with my parents' initial opposition and stuff like that," he said.

"Yeah, it all happened like in the movies. All that makes me happy is that we are together and we will be so forever," she said, taking a deep breath.

"You know, I thank Uncle Louis for being there for me. I don't know what I would have done if I was only surrounded by conservative people who behave as if we were still in the nineteenth century. Those people are a hard nut to crack if you ask me" he said, yawning. He heard his wife not responding. When he checked she was fast asleep. She looked so beautiful, he thought.

Thus, from the rubble of cynicism and bigotry grew a tree of love that would bear the fruits of freedom. The rays of emancipation and reconciliation were borne by the two lovers. Their relationship epitomised nation building epoch fraught with a myriad of problems.

12

Twenty years passed and the two lovers were still madly in love. They were blessed with four children, two girls and two boys. Deborah, the first born, was a second year medicine student. Piet Jr was in Grade 11 at one of the most expensive private schools in the country. Rampho Jr and Freedom Mampho were doing Grades 7 and 4 respectively at the local public school.

Funkel had obtained his PhD in Nuclear Science and Mpho had a Master of Laws (LLM) degree. She had opened her own legal agency.

Everything seemed to be working according to plan until one day:

"I wonder why I always feel so weak nowadays," said Mpho.

"You need to check your sugar level or other diseases, Mom," said Deborah, "it could be a symptom of something serious. People should not fear consulting their doctors whenever anything unusual happens to their bodies."

"Oh! Is it the doctor talking?" Mpho asked rhetorically.

"Of course, Mom," said Deborah jokingly.

"You are right my child. We wait until it is too late before we consult a doctor," Mpho said.

"Old age is also knocking. That is why the elderly always feel tired. Our immune system weakens with age," said Deborah.

"You are going to be a brilliant doctor," said Mpho, "I am proud of you my baby," she said, stroking her hand.

"Of course Mom, I take after the best. You and Dad are great. How could you make a stupid child," she said.

That night Mpho asked her husband Funkel to accompany her to a doctor for blood test.

"Why do you want to do this really?" asked Funkel.

"It's just that I have not been feeling well recently. I thought it was work related fatigue but it persists even when I am on leave," said Mpho. Funkel kept quiet for a while as if pondering what his wife had said.

"All right, my love. I will take you there tomorrow. I am on leave for a week. I have all the time in the world to attend to you my beautiful wife," he said.

They went to the family doctor who drew Mpho's blood and advised her to take extended leave from work as he suspected that she was developing symptoms of stress.

The whole family went to church on that Sunday. The priest taught about trying times in people's lives. He said the devil was opportunistic because he targeted those who seemed happy and obeying the Lord. He told the congregation, "It is at this point where the children of God should be steadfast and show their faith in their Creator," he said to a deafening Amen, from the members.

Mpho felt sanctified by the preacher. Her poor health was a trial by the devil that was determined to destroy her faith in God.

The results of the tests were due, so Mpho went to the doctor to hear the diagnosis.

"You should have come with your husband Mrs Koekemoer. Is he around perhaps?" inquired the doctor.

"No. I came alone, he went to work. Is there a problem? Mpho asked anxiously.

"I am afraid there is, even though we cannot be certain at this juncture. We need to make another test and this time your husband must also test," said the doctor.

"Doctor you are scaring me. It sounds as if I am about to die. What disease is this that needs my husband to take a blood test as well? I have never heard him complain about anything. He seems as healthy as a horse," said Mpho, sounding a little hysterical.

"No need to worry Madam. It is not anything that cannot be controlled. If it becomes a reality, it will be controlled. I am only glad that you came when you did. It is at its early stage of development. Hopefully our fears might be proved wrong with our second test. No need to worry though. I will draw your blood in the meantime and your husband's will be drawn when he comes in. The sooner that is done, the better," said the doctor, trying to maintain a reassuring gesture.

Mpho looked devastated. She said a silent prayer and asked God to spare her for the sake of her children who needed a mother to guide them through difficult times.

On her arrival at home she called her husband to come home as soon as possible.

When Funkel arrived he found his wife in tears. It was a mammoth task to calm her down to explain what was wrong.

"How could this have happened to me? I am a faithful woman for heaven's sake. I haven't had any other man in my life besides you. You must have an explanation for all this," said Mpho, in tears.

"What do I have to explain? What did the doctor say?" asked Funkel, who seemed confused.

"Tell me, are you cheating on me?" asked Mpho.

"What kind of a question is that?" asked Funkel.

"I am asking you because there is no way I can be HIV positive if you are not sleeping around," said Mpho.

"What? You are... I don't believe that," said Funkel.

"The doctor wants you to come for tests as well. You must go there right now," said Mpho.

"I cannot be HIV positive. I am not cheating on you. If I am, you would be responsible for it. Who knows, you could have slipped once or twice with your lawyer or judge colleagues. If I find that I am positive I am going to kill you," said Funkel, pointing a threatening finger at Mpho.

"I have never cheated on you. Maybe you were seduced by the sluts at the university where you are working," said Mpho, defending herself.

Funkel stormed out of the room and went straight to the doctor's surgery for tests. He didn't want to do instant tests. He insisted on thorough laboratory tests. He then went to a bar where he drowned himself in alcohol.

There were strained relations between Funkel and Mpho. The two leaked the bad news to their families who hastened to accuse their counterparts of raising a loose child who had made their own well-raised pay the ultimate price. Racial slurs exploded like cluster bombs where the homes of the affected turned into battle fields.

Mpho went to church daily and prayed for hours on end. The priest knew her problems and was supportive. He would pay the Koekemoer family a visit once a week to offer his guidance.

They asked for other tests after a period of three months had elapsed. During that period they were sleeping in different bedrooms. Those true lovers had become sworn enemies. They hardly looked each other in the eyes.

Their fighting was taking a toll on their children. They were torn between their parents. They loved them both. They could not take sides. They joined their mother in prayers and attended church whenever they had the opportunity.

The priest had a mammoth task trying to reconcile the Koekemoers. "It is at times like this where you need one another the most. You must have faith in the miracles and greatness of God so that He should provide. If you walk in God's light you will never experience darkness. Have faith my children, God will give you the right answer at His own time," he would say.

Peace and love gradually returned to the family of the Koekemoers. Laughter could once again be heard several streets from their house. All the pastor could say was, "Praise the Lord!"

The End.

Glossary:

Boer seun	= Afrikaner boy.
Boet	= big brother.
Chomza	= a friend.
Klein baas	= a young boss.
Magadi	= a bride's price paid by the groom.
Mannetjie	= a young man.
Meisie	= a girl.
Muti	= medicinal herbs.
Ossewa	= ox-wagon
Paps	= father.
Sangoma	= traditional doctor.
Siya vuma	= we agree.
Vumani	= agree.
Wena	= You.
Yebo	= yes

****

www.ingramcontent.com/pod-product-compliance
Lightning Source LLC
Chambersburg PA
CBHW051244170626
46809CB00004B/1486

* 9 780099 223020 *